TAMMY and the PHARMACIST

By
Beatrice E. Toppins

Copyright © 2007 by Beatrice E. Toppins

Tammy and the Pharmacist
by Beatrice E. Toppins

Printed in the United States of America

ISBN 978-1-60266-140-0

All rights reserved solely by the author. The author guarantees all contents are original and do not infringe upon the legal rights of any other person or work. No part of this book may be reproduced in any form without the permission of the author. The views expressed in this book are not necessarily those of the publisher.

Unless otherwise indicated, Bible quotations are taken from King James Version of the Bible. Copyright © 1998 by Holman Bible Publishers Nashville, Tennessee.

Cast of Characters:

Howard Peters
Ella Peters
Dorothy Peters
Tammy Waring
Tina Waring
Robert Green
Pastor 'Bob' Harrington
David Williams
Valerie Williams
Tom Adkins
Lucy Tomlinson
Mary and Donald Anderson
Bert Lansing

John Roberts
Martha Andrews
Cindy Lawson
Don Lawson-board member

www.xulonpress.com

Author Biography:

From the time I was able to read, I have had a love affair with books. Some books I have read at least three times. My favorite authors are John Grisham, Tim LaHaye, Tommy Tenney who wrote 'One Night with the King' which recently was made into a movie. Also Benny Hinn and Oral Roberts. I have written several books, one of which I made into a screen-play with Final Draft, and which is registered with the Writer's Guild East in New York City. I intend rewriting it and having it printed as a novel instead. Also, I am working on a sequel to 'Tammy and the Pharmacist' which should be ready in a few months.

I am ninety-two now and my doctor says I'll probably live to be one hundred or more. God has been good to me and I believe He is the real author of this book. We have had a lot of fun together writing it!

Beatrice E. Toppins

CHAPTER ONE

Howard Peters inserted his key into the front door of his building. He'd been a pharmacist in the small town of Glendale, Arizona for almost fifteen years. Knew practically everyone in town, he did. Yep, a guy gets to be almost as necessary as the doctor, he thought proudly. He surveyed his reflection in the fountain mirror with satisfaction. Grinning, he reached up and patted the wavy brown hair that swept back from his forehead. Executing a soft-shoe over to the cosmetic counter, he lifted the dust cover and began to fold it. Just then the doorbell pealed as a customer entered. Straightening up, dignity fell on him like a cloak as he turned to greet her.

"Good Morning, Hannah, you're out bright and early. What can I do for you?"

"Well, I knew you were going to New York today and I wanted to get my prescription filled before you left."

"Tom could have done that for you, Hannah."

'I know he could. I just wanted you to do it."

"It's nice to know people have confidence in you. I'll have it ready for you in about five minutes."

Meanwhile, his wife, Ella and her neighbor, Iris were having coffee in Ella's kitchen. "How come you don't go to New York with Howard?"

"Well, for one thing, I can't leave Dorothy home alone. She's too young for that. For another, I'm nor really interested in shopping for things like that. Howard knows the sort of things his customers like. I'd just be in the way."

"Maybe so," responded Iris, "but if I was Howard, I'd want you to take an interest in what I do. Well, guess I'd better get on home or I'll never get any work done." So saying, she went out the kitchen door.

Just then, Howard's twelve year old daughter came bursting in the front door., letting the screen door slam behind her. "Hi, Mom, is Daddy home yet? I wanna ask him if I can go to New York with him."

"Now, Dorothy, we've been over all this before! You know you can't go and that's that!"

"You just don't want me to go with Daddy." She pouted. He likes to take me places. We have fun together."

Just then a car door slammed. "There's Daddy now. I'll ask him and see what he says." Howard entered. Dorothy threw herself at him. "Daddy, please say I can go to New York with you."

Howard picked her up and swung her around then put her down, puffing with the unaccustomed exercise. "Whew, you're getting to be quite a chunk. Can't do that much anymore. And, no, you can't go to New York this time but tell you what I'll do. Next time I go I'll take both you and your Mom so you can be company for each other. How's that?"

"Oh, Daddy, that's a wonderful idea. Ooh, I love you so much."

"And I love both you and your Mom. Now I must get going. I have a plane to catch at two-thirty."

"Lunch is ready." Ella said, "and I have your luggage all packed and ready to go." She put their lunch on the table and they sat down to eat. Then Howard hugged and kissed both of them, picked up his briefcase and his suitcase and hurried out to the car, which he planned on leaving at the terminal.

CHAPTER TWO

Arriving at the airport, he left his car in the parking lot and hurried to the main gate just as the announcer was calling, "Gate 23 for New York now boarding."

"Whew." Howard cried. "I almost missed it. I just made it."

Finding his seat, he stuffed his luggage in the overhead unit, then sat back and relaxed to watch the movie. Suddenly, the movie was interrupted by a news program. Israel and the Hezbollah in Lebanon were fighting! Many innocent people had been killed. Howard remembered the day when the terrorists had used jets to bomb the twin World Trade Towers in New York, the famous 9-11 Massacre! He turned to his seat partner to comment on the news. She was weeping.

"I'm sorry! Are you all right?" he asked.

"Yes, I'm all right but my husband is over there on business so, naturally, I'm worried about him."

"Have you heard from him recently?" he asked.

"Yes", he called me yesterday and said they were trying to get all Americans out. That's why I'm flying to New York. I'm supposed to meet him there. I just hope he made it out."

"I'm sure he'll be all right. If there's anything I can do just let me know. I'll be at the Hilton. My name is Howard Peters. I own a pharmacy in Glendale, Arizona. I'm on a shopping trip for the business.

You say you are flying to New York to meet your husband. May I ask where you are from?"

"Actually, not too far from where you live. We live in Mesa, Arizona. I have friends in Long Island and I'll be staying with them. My name is Valerie Williams. If you wish, I'll call and leave a message for you as soon as I hear from my husband. I thank you for your interest."

"You're welcome. It's the least anyone could do. Hmm, It looks like the plane is beginning to descend. We should be in New York soon."

The plane continued its descent and soon the skyscrapers of New York appeared on the skyline. As it approached the airport, the stewardess warned everyone to fasten their seatbelts and put their seats in an upright position. Soon they had taxied to the Jet-way corridor that was attached to the gate through which they would be departing. Howard assisted his partner to get her things together and then gathered his own.

"Thank you for your help. As soon as I hear from my husband, I'll call your hotel and leave a message for you. Thank you again."

CHAPTER THREE

Howard had settled in his hotel room and was immersed in the work for which he had come to New York City. Such goods as he was shopping for was the 'icing on the cake' when it came to drug stores during the holiday season. More than his partner, he had a natural instinct for knowing what his customers would like for gifts as well as things they would like for themselves, just because they came from New York.

Right now he stood looking over an assortment of fountains that were especially popular this season. Suddenly he felt an odd sensation and, looking up, he found a pair of striking blue eyes smiling at him.

"You don't remember me, do you?" the blue eyes queried.

Howard looked at the blond hair that framed her oval face, the delicately tinted lips, the small turned up nose and he frowned thoughtfully, "Should I?"

Her eyes sparkled with mischief, "Not really, I guess. I'm Tammy Waring. I was two years behind you in high school. I had a crush on you when you played fullback on the football squad."

"Now, I remember," Howard cried delightedly, "but you had braces on your teeth and wore your hair in pigtails! No wonder I didn't recognize you. What are you doing in New York?"

"Oh, I live here," She replied. "I work at Macy's in the audit department. What are you doing in New York?"

"I'm on a buying trip for a drugstore that Tom Adkins and I own in Glendale." He said as he studied her pretty face. "Look, do you have time for lunch? I was just going to eat. Maybe we could have lunch together."

"Gee, I'm sorry. I just had lunch and I have to be back to work at one. Where are you staying? I'll call you and maybe we can get together for dinner."

"Hey, I'd like that! I'm at the Hilton. Call me around five. I should be back by then."

"I'll do that." Tammy replied. "Bye now, I gotta run."

Howard whistled jauntily as he wended his way toward the cafeteria on the corner. "Imagine a gorgeous creature like Tammy having a crush on me," he said to himself.

Later, he was just emerging from the shower, a huge towel wrapped around his torso, when the phone rang. He caught his big toe on the leg of a chair and hopped painfully about as he lifted the receiver. "Hello?"

"Hi, this is Tammy. You sound upset. Is something the matter?

"No, I just banged my big toe on a chair and it sure hurts."

"I'm sorry," she said.

"That's okay. Now, let me take you out to dinner. And maybe a show afterward."

"Well, okay" said Tammy. "Pick me up at six o'clock at 648 14th Street, Apartment 3, only no movie after dinner. I have someplace else that I'd like to go. Alright?"

"Yeah, just a minute. Let me write that down, 648 14th Street, apartment 3, right? See you about six, okay?"

"Yes. That'll be fine."

He phoned a cab to pick him up at five-forty –five then hurried to finish getting dressed. His heart hammered at the audacity of the date he was looking forward to. What would Ella think if she knew? At least Tammy didn't ask him to her apartment, he mused.

She was waiting when the cab drove up in front of her apartment.

Howard gave further directions to the driver then turned his attention to Tammy. "My you look lovely. You know, we have so much to talk about. I don't even know if you 're married or have children or anything. Tell me about your self."

"I was married," she replied, "but my husband was killed in a train wreck last year. He was on a business trip and two trains collided head-on."

"Oh, yes, I did read about that. Of course, I had no idea that anyone I knew was involved. Oh, here we are. We'll have to continue our talk at dinner." He paid the cabbie and helped Tammy alight.

In the restaurant, the head-waiter seated them in a remote corner. Candlelight flickered in the light breeze that emanated from the air-conditioner. Soft music filled the air that seemed to enfold them in an aura of quiet happiness. Howard ordered for both of them, then said to Tammy, "You were telling me about the train wreck."

"There isn't really a whole lot more to tell. Jim was killed instantly. Both legs were severed and there were internal injuries. I was thankful he died. He was spared any suffering. He wouldn't have wanted to live that way. He was a Christian so I know he's with the Lord. That's a great comfort to me."

Howard reached out his hand to cover hers in a comforting esture. She allowed it to remain for a minute, then withdrew hers gently. Howard seemed not to notice as she asked, "How about you? Are you married?"

"Yes, I married Ella Peabody from Scottsdale. We have a little girl, Dorothy, who is twelve years old."

"Yes, I do remember Ella. She and I are about the same age,

I, too, have a little girl, Tina. She lives with her grandmother in up state New York. I see her as often as I can but, working like I do, I can't provide a proper home for her."

Just then their dinner arrived. Tammy bowed her head in silent prayer but Howard appeared not to notice as he busied himself with his napkin and silverware.

"You mentioned someplace else you'd rather go than to a movie,"

Howard remarked after she lifted her head. "Are you going to let me in on the secret now?"

"No," she said. "It's a place not far from here but I'm sure you'll enjoy the evening. Just trust me. Okay?"

"Okay," Howard replied, his hopes for a quiet evening with Tammy fading away. "Whatever you say."

CHAPTER FOUR

Their dinner over, they gathered their wraps and wended their way to the street. Howard started to hail a cab but Tammy said, "Please, do you mind if we walk? It's not far and it's so nice out."

"Of course," he said as they turned their footsteps northward. After a few blocks they came to a small brick building. Howard heard music and singing. "Dear God, she's taking me to some kind of meeting," he muttered to himself.

Turning in at the doorway, they entered a large room where Tammy was immediately surrounded by a host of friends, "Where were you?" they cried. "We almost started without you!"

"Let me introduce you to my friend," she said, as she pulled Howard forward. "This is an old friend from back home, Howard Peters. "

"Happy to meet you, sir, welcome," came from many lips as they surged toward him to welcome him. There was much hand shaking, then Tammy led Howard forward to a seat near the front.

"I hope you won't mind," she said, "but I'm in charge of the music." The musicians: a guitar player, a keyboard player and a saxophonist began to play. Tammy began to sing and the group joined in. The words were unfamiliar to Howard so he just listened but he was impressed with the quality of the music. He did figure out that the title of the song was 'Nothing Is Impossible With God'.

When the song was ended, Tammy remained standing, then began to sing a solo, 'I'd Rather Have Jesus." As she finished the song, the group sat with bowed heads, praying and worshipping Jesus.

Then, the young man who was leader of the group stood to his feet. "If there is anyone here who needs a closer walk with Jesus or who has never accepted Him as your Savior, just lift your hand and we'll be glad to pray with you."

Somehow Howard felt his hand going up. The group gathered around him and began to pray. As they prayed, Howard gave his life to Jesus and began to rejoice with the others. He turned to Tammy, his voice tremulous, and thanked her for bringing him.

Tammy, tears streaming down her face, nodded and took his hand to lead him out as the group said their good-nights.

Howard hailed a cab and took Tammy home. "Goodnight, Tammy, and God bless you. And thank you once again for not being ashamed to take me to that meeting. I believe God led you to do it."

"Goodnight to you, too. I hope you'll be able to bring your wife and daughter to the Lord and many, many others may come to know the Lord because of your testimony."

CHAPTER FIVE

Howard went back to his hotel, but not to sleep. He pondered on the change that had occurred in his life and what effect it would have on Ella and Dorothy when he told them. He hadn't brought a Bible with him or even thought of such a thing, but he remembered seeing a Gideon Bible in the night stand drawer. He reached over and lifted it out and began to read. It had been so long since he had even picked up the Bible that he wasn't sure where to start but the Lord knew where to take him and he opened the Bible to John 3:16. "For God so loved the world that He gave his only begotten Son that whosoever believeth on Him should not perish but have everlasting life!"

"Thank you, Father," Howard prayed. "That was just what I needed." He then climbed in to bed and was soon fast asleep."

The next morning, Howard awakened early. Remembering his experience from the night before, he reached for the Bible and opened it to the chapter he had been reading. Turning back to the first chapter of John, he began to read. "In the beginning was the Word, and the Word was with God, and the Word was God. 'How can that be?" he wondered. "Word is capitalized. That means that the Word is a person! It also says that he was with God and that he was God. How amazing! Does that mean that Jesus is the Word and that he is also God?"

He dropped to his knees beside the bed and bowed his head before the Lord. "Father, it has been so long since I have really talked to you. Please forgive me and help me to understand your word. Help me to comprehend what you mean by the words I have just read that I may know how to worship you properly. It seems to me, that you, Father and Jesus, the Word, and the Holy Spirit are ONE! Am I correct in assuming that? I feel in my heart that it is so. Please direct my thoughts and use me to reach others. Guide me into all truth that I may be an instrument in thy hands to reach my loved ones and others at home. Bless Tammy and her daughter and mother and supply their needs. In the blessed and Holy name of Jesus, I pray. Amen."

He rose from his knees and began to make preparations for his shopping trip that day. He was almost ready to leave his room when the phone rang. "I wonder who could be calling at this hour." He lifted the receiver. "Hello?"

"Good morning, Howard. How are you this morning?"

"Good morning, to you, too, Tammy. I'm fine. I just read an amazing statement in the Bible from John, chapter 1, the very first verse about the beginning. Then I bowed on my knees beside the bed and talked to the Lord about what I had just read. I feel like I want to go out and convert the whole world, especially to go home and witness to my family and friends. Thank you for taking me to that meeting."

"Oh, I'm so happy to hear you say that! I hope you'll keep in touch when you go back home. I'm anxious to hear

how your family will react. I must go now as I have to be at my desk in about three minutes. I'll call you this evening. Bye."

Howard had just hung up the phone when it rang again.

"Hello?"

"This is the front desk. A message was left here for you. Would you like me to read it to you or would you prefer to pick it up"

"Yes, please read it to me and then I'll pick up a copy on my way out," Howard responded.

"Very well. This is the message. "Dear Mr. Peters. I'm happy to inform you that my husband arrived safely late last night. Thank you for caring. Valerie Williams.

'Thank you, sir.", Howard said.

"You're welcome, I'll have a copy ready for you."

Tammy and the Pharmacist

Howard took his briefcase and closed the door behind him as he walked to the elevator. On the main floor, he walked to the desk to pick up his message, then turned and walked back to the small café where he planned on having breakfast. Seating himself in a booth, he opened the message and was pleasantly surprised to see that Valerie had enclosed her address on Long Island and a phone number. Beckoning a waiter, he asked if he could have a phone at the booth. Nodding his head, the waiter brought a phone and plugged it in for him."

"Would you like to order now?" the waiter inquired.

"Yes. I would and thank you for the phone."

The waiter opened his pad, "We have a special breakfast menu this morning, sir. Two eggs, any style, 2 sausages, 2 pancakes with maple syrup, your choice of juices and or coffee.

"That sounds great." Howard replied, "I'll have the eggs over light, sausages well done, cranberry juice (if you have it) and coffee with cream."

"It shall be as you wish, including the cranberry juice. I take it you want the pancakes, also?"

"Yes, of course. Howard replied. Then taking the message from his pocket, he dialed the numbers on it and was pleased to hear Valerie's voice answer the phone.

"Hello?'

"Good morning, this is Howard Peters. I am so glad your husband arrived safely. Thank you for calling to let me know."

"Oh, thank you! He's right here. Would you like to speak to him?"

"Certainly."

"Good morning, sir. This is David Williams. I wish to thank you for reassuring my wife last night on the plane. Perhaps we can meet sometime. I'd like to get to know you."

"I plan on finishing shopping for my business today and flying home tomorrow. I understand you live near Glendale, Arizona.

"Why, yes, we do! We live in Mesa. Does Valerie have your home address?

Tammy and the Pharmacist

"I don't think so but I'll be glad to give it to you. I believe this is your home address that she left at the desk, telling me that you had arrived. Is that correct?"

"Yes, it is. Thank you for your kindness to my wife. We'll keep in touch."

"Glad I could help. I'll keep in touch, too. Just in case, this is my home address.23174 Lancaster Blvd., Glendale, Arizona. I do hope to see you one of these days. Unfortunately, my plane leaves at 7:30 tomorrow morning and I still have a lot more shopping to do today. Call me when you get home and we'll get together for a barbecue or something. Ok?

"Thank you. We'll do that. Good bye for now."

As he hung up, Howard took the message he had gotten at the desk and put it in a safe place in his briefcase. He purposed in his heart to follow through and lead these people to Christ, too, if they didn't already know Him.

He had just finished his conversation when his breakfast arrived. Bowing his head, he gave thanks to his Heavenly Father, then began to eat his meal.

Knowing he wouldn't be able to take much on the plane he had ordered everything to be shipped except for personal items that he had purchased for his family.

Later, his shopping done, he packed everything he would be taking on the plane, leaving only the outfit he would need in the morning.

Once again, he decided to eat dinner in his room so he'd be sure to be there when Tammy called. And he planned on calling Ella, too. He had called the dining room and ordered dinner, earlier. There was a knock at the door and the waiter was there with his dinner. He wheeled in a cart with the dinner tastefully arranged, a small bud vase with a single rose in it gave it a festive air but the aroma was what really turned him on as he gave the waiter a tip, then turned to seat himself at the small table, He bowed his head to give thanks to his Heavenly Father. "Dear Heavenly Father, Thank you again for your blessings to me today. Thank you for the friends I've met. May I be able to reach each .one for thee. And, Father, please do something about the situation in Lebanon. So many innocent people are being killed. Help our President to know what to do, Amen

He had barely finished when the phone rang. "That must be Tammy," he murmured as he reached for the phone. "Hello."\

"Hi, I'm glad I caught you. I thought you might be out for dinner."

"No, I wanted to finish packing and get ready for morning so I had the hotel send dinner up. Then, too, I didn't want to miss your call."

"Thank you. I'm glad. What time does your plane leave?"

"7:30 A.M. That means I have to get up with the birds"

"Wow! That means you'll have to get up at least by six." Tammy exclaimed. " I guess I'd better not tie up your line too long. Have you called Ella yet?"

"No, I haven't had time. I'll call her right after we hang up.. By the way, have you had a vacation yet this year?"

"No. Why do you ask?"

"I thought you might want to come out and visit sometime. You and your daughter and maybe your mother."

"I don't think we could. Mom couldn't afford it and neither can I. It's awfully nice of you to think of it, though."

"Well, when is it? If we can find a way to make it happen?"

"The closest thing to a vacation would have to be between Christmas and New Years, so I hardly think that would be possible."

"Do you remember the young woman I told you about who was crying on the plane here? Well, I talked with both her and her husband (he did make it safely from Lebanon) and they live close to where we live. Maybe between us, we can make it possible. What a Christmas that would be!"

"I can see you're a dreamer. I guess this is something we'll have to leave with the Lord! If it's His will, we'll be happy to come."

"Now that's the way I like to hear you talk. I'm sure Ella will be happy, too. She likes parties and this would be a BIG ONE! And now that I have the Lord in my life, we'll just leave it with Him."

"That I can do. The Word says 'Take your burdens to the Lord and leave them there.' Now, I guess I'd better get off the line so you can call Ella. Say 'hello' to her for me. 'Bye."

'Bye. We'll be in touch with you. Do you have a computer? What about e-mail?"

"Sorry, that's something I don't have at home and I think Macy's would frown on me using theirs on the job. Goodnight."

"Goodnight and God bless you." Tammy hung up the phone reluctantly.

Howard replaced the receiver and sat a moment in prayer. Then took the phone and dialed his number at home. When the phone rang his daughter answered it. "Hello?"

"Dorothy. This is Daddy. Is mother there?"

"Yes, Daddy, just a moment. I'll call her."

"Mom, Daddy's on the phone."

"Hello, Howard. I was expecting your call. When will you be home?"

"About one o'clock tomorrow. My plane leaves at 7:30 A.M. I have a lot to tell you. Can't wait to see you. I'll tell you all about it when I get home."

"We're glad you're coming home, too. We miss you when you're gone. I love you. Good-bye."

Howard hung up the phone, turned off the TV and the lights and went to take his shower before climbing into bed for a good night's sleep. Remembering his experience the previous night, he knelt beside the bed and poured out his heart to the Lord. "Dear Father in Heaven, I come before you again to seek guidance for the coming weeks ahead. I know I should have waited to ask Ella before I invited Tammy and her family for Christmas. Will you please smooth the way for me? I don't want anything to hinder my testimony to Ella or any of our family and friends. I want to win them all for thee. Please remember Valerie and her husband, David. May I have a chance to witness to them, too. In Jesus precious name, I ask it. Amen."

CHAPTER SIX

Howard had left a request at the main desk for a 'wake-up' call at five A.M. but he was already awake. He called for breakfast to be sent up, then dressed as he waited. He also called the front desk for a porter to come up and take his parcels and luggage down to the front entrance. He finished his breakfast, then followed the porter down to the cab that was waiting for him. He just barely made it to the airport in time to hear the announcer calling that the plane for Sky Harbor in Phoenix was at gate.15. 'Whew," he said to himself, "I've got to quit cutting my time so close! " Giving his ticket to the attendant at the gate, he entered the Jet-way and followed the other passengers on to the plane. Finding his seat, he loaded his carry-on luggage in the overhead compartment and settled down in his seat next to the window, figuring on taking a few hours' nap. A middle-aged man and his wife took the seats next to him. He nodded his head to them in greeting, then closed his eyes hoping to nap.

The plane was revving its engines, preparing for take-off. Suddenly, there was a sharp crash and a burst of lightening as a thunderstorm brewed overhead. The stewardess stood up to calm the people and said it would be a few minutes before take-off until the storm was over. Howard bowed his head in silent prayer asking God to calm the elements. It was not long until the storm was over and the plane was once more able to rev its engine preparatory to take-off. Because several planes had been lined up for take-off it was several minutes before their plane could get clearance to go ahead. Soon the plane was aloft and had risen above the clouds so there was no more turbulence.

The passenger in the seat next to him said to Howard. " I noticed you bowed your head in prayer when the storm hit. Are you a Christian?"

"Why, yes, I am. I went to church all my life but I never really knew the Lord until the other night. A young woman I used to know in High School took me to a meeting and when a young man stood and asked if anyone there needed to know the Lord, I found my hand going up. They surrounded and prayed for me and I became a 'born again' Christian. Now I want to tell the whole world about Jesus. Do you know Him?"

"Why, yes, I do. My wife, too, is a Christian. We pastor a church in Phoenix."

"That's great! The first thing I want to do when I get home is tell my wife about that experience. Maybe we can visit your church."

"You will surely be welcome. Here's my card with the church's address and phone number. Do you live in Phoenix?"

"No, my partner and I own a drug store in Glendale so, naturally, we live there."

"That's not far from our church. I hope you'll be able to bring your family and join us,.."

"I see your name is Harrington. Are you any relation to Tom Harrington that converted a hospital in California into a shelter for the homeless?"

'Why, yes, I'm his father.

"Wow! I've heard a lot about you. I can't wait until I can begin to witness to people and tell them how much Jesus loves them!"

"Well, if you come and worship with us, I'm sure you will soon be involved in that kind of testimony because we don't limit our testimony to those in church but try to witness wherever there is an opportunity just like the young lady who took you to that meeting."

"I'll surely try to convince my wife that it's God's will for us to attend the church where you pastor. There's another young couple that I want to witness to. The husband was in Lebanon when this war broke out. He was fortunate to be one of those who were evacuated. He had called his wife and asked her to meet him in New York. She was weeping so I asked her if I could help. I gave her my name and told her where I was staying. She said she would call and leave a message at the desk if her husband arrived. She did call and leave a message at the desk that her husband had arrived safely. As a result I was able to talk to both of them and found out that they also lived in Arizona in Mesa. There wasn't time to get together then but we plan on doing that when they are back home."

"That's wonderful. Sounds like the Lord has you right on track already. Let me know if I can be of any help."

"I sure will. I can hardly wait to tell my wife and daughter."

"I'll be praying for you. Guess we'd better get our things together. We'll be landing in a few minutes."

"Thank you. I'm sure you'll be seeing more of us, — Oh, here's my card. Call me any time and drop in if you're in the vicinity."

CHAPTER SEVEN

"I'll do that. They gathered their luggage as the plane landed and went up the aisle to disembark.

Howard hurried to the parking lot to get his car, stowed everything in the trunk and was soon on his way home.

Driving into the garage, he unloaded his luggage and carried it through to the kitchen. "Hi, I'm home," he called.

Dorothy came running with Ella right behind her.

"Hi, Daddy," she said as she wrapped her arms around his neck.

Holding on to Dorothy, he wrapped his other arm around Ella as he kissed her. "Boy, I'm sure glad to be home. Have I got a lot to tell you."

"You must have had a good time," Ella replied.

"Oh, I did! I got a lot of nice things for the store and I'm having them shipped. I brought a few things home for both of you but wait till I tell you my news."

"Let's go in the living room and sit down so you can relax while you tell us," Ella replied.

Howard lowered his arms and followed them to the iving room. He and Ella sat on the sofa and Dorothy sat on the floor at his feet.

"Now, what did you do that was so exciting?"

"Well, first of all, I had gone to a warehouse and done some of my shopping so I could have things shipped direct. Then I was looking in a window at some other things when I looked up and saw a young woman smiling at me. Finally, I turned around and asked her, "Should I know you?"

Tammy and the Pharmacist

"She said, yes, I'm Tammy Waring. I used to be two grades behind you in high school. Do you remember her?"

"Oh, yes, I remember Tammy."

"Well, I didn't know her because back then she had braces on her teeth and wore her hair in pig-tails. She didn't look the same at all. I asked if she'd have lunch with me and she said she'd already had lunch and she had to be back at work at Macy's .so I suggested I take her to dinner and maybe a movie."

"She agreed to go out to dinner but said she had someplace else she'd rather go after dinner so I said OK. During dinner, I asked if she was married and if she had any children. She said she had been married but her husband was killed in a train wreck. Do you remember when we read about that terrible train wreck in the paper about a year ago? Well, that's the one her husband was killed in. She also has a girl about the same age as Dorothy named Tina who lives with her grandmother in upper New York state. She says she can't keep her with her because she has to work. Anyway, when we got near the building where we were headed, I heard music and singing. I muttered to myself. 'Dear God, she's taking me to some kind of a meeting." Turns out, she was the song leader. She started out leading them in a song, then stepped up to the mike and began to sing a solo. It was called "I'd rather have Jesus."

"Then a young man got up and gave a talk about giving your heart to Jesus. When he asked if there was anyone there who didn't know Jesus or had gotten far away from him to raise their hands and they would pray for him. I didn't even have to think about it but found myself lifting my hand in the air. The group all came around me and prayed for me and I gave my heart to Jesus. Then they all came around me. Everyone had tears running down their faces, even Tammy had tears streaming down her face and I thanked her for bringing me there. So-o, you have a new Daddy and a new Husband!" By then, Dorothy and Ella were weeping, too.

"I never thought I'd hear you talk like this. " Ella said.

"That isn't all" Howard said. "On the way home on the plane, I met a man whose son is the one who made a home for the homeless out of a hospital in California. I asked this man if he knew that man and he said, "Yes, I'm his father." Turns out he and his wife pastor a huge church in Phoenix! He invited us to come there to church. Would you like to go?

"We might try it but I would miss all my friends where we go now. Can we wait and see? This is all so new to me."

"Yes, I can see it would be. We'll just have to take it one step at a time."

"I'd like to try it, Daddy. It sounds exciting. I wish we could see Tammy's daughter. It must be lonely for her. I'd miss you and Mom terribly if I didn't have either one of you like Tammy's daughter."

"Well, maybe we can go once a month or every other Sunday. That way we'd have friends in both places." Howard replied.

"I think that's a great idea, don't you, Mom?" Dorothy said.

"About Tammy's daughter," said Howard, "I felt sorry about her, too. So I asked Tammy if they could come out and spend a week for a vacation between Christmas and New Years. I know I should have asked you first, Ella, but I was feeling so sorry for them. Do you mind, if we can find a way for them to come? She doesn't have any money besides her living expenses, but I met some other people that you'll be getting acquainted with as they live in Mesa. He was in Lebanon and was evacuated just this last Friday. His wife flew on the same plane with me. In fact, she sat next to me and she was crying. I asked if there was anything I could do. She said not but she would call and let me know if her husband got there safe. She did leave a message that he had arrived safely and left an address and phone number. I called and was able to talk to her husband. We'll be getting together, too."

"This is all so strange to me. I never saw you like this before! You'll have to give me time to digest all this. Please be patient with me. Okay?"

"Yes, of course. I just couldn't hold it all in. I've never been like this before either. What a stodgy Christian I must have been. No fire, no caring, just going along with the crowd. But you'll get used to it and you'll like it. Maybe you'll even get excited like I am."

"I don't know about Mom, Daddy, but I'm getting real excited and I want you to tell me all about that meeting you went to. I'd like to go to a meeting like that."

"I'm quite sure if we go to Pastor Harrington's church that it will be like that. I understand that they break up into cell groups and meet in different neighborhoods. We might even end up having our own group right here in our neighborhood."

"You mean you *might even become a preacher?*"

"I don't really know. You have to be called by God to be a preacher. All I know is that I want to tell everybody I see how to become a real Christian."

"Dinner is almost ready. Could we eat now and talk some more later?" Ella asked.

"Sure", Howard replied. "What are we having?"

"One of your favorites. Sweet and sour meat balls with pineapple and green peppers over brown rice, a salad, hot rolls and apple pie."

"Mmn, mmn, sounds delicious. Lead me to it."

Ella dished up the meal and placed it on the table. As they sat down to the table, Howard bowed his head to give thanks. Ella and Dorothy both looked startled but quickly folded their hands in prayer as Howard prayed. "Father, we thank you tonight for this food and all the blessings you have poured out upon us. May we use the strength we receive from it to work for your glory. Amen."

"You sure have changed a lot in the last few days "Ella commented. But I think I like it. It makes you more exciting."

"I'm glad you feel that way. It *is* exciting! I didn't realize how exciting working for God could be. When we have finished dinner, I have something else I want to institute as 'head of the family' and that is family worship."

"What is that?" Dorothy cried.

"That's when we all get our Bibles and read the Word of God and discuss what we have read means and how we can apply it to our lives, and how we can show it to others that they may find it, too. I'd like to start it tonight so when dinner is done we can clear the table, sit around it and read God's word and pray that it will be fulfilled in our lives. Also, we can pray for people like Tammy and her family and others like them. We can also join a prayer chain so that when people are in need of healing or other problems in their lives they can call us for prayer. Having family worship will give us the strength to do whatever God calls us to do and He will provide the means. That's another thing God has shown me. We need to tithe."

"What is that?" piped up Dorothy.

"Tithing is giving ten per cent of all your income. That's the least. It belongs to God. You aren't really giving until you give more. For instance, you receive five dollars a week. Fifty cents of that belongs to God. You're not giving anything until you give more than that."

"Wow! That doesn't leave much, does it Daddy?"

"Not by your standards but as you give more God gives you more. You can't out-give God!"

"You know, Daddy, we learn about some of this stuff in Sunday School but I'm anxious to read it right out of the Bible, like you do. Will you help me?"

"I sure will. Let's finish our dinner and we can get started right away. I have a scripture that both you and your Mom will find exciting:"

Finishing their dinner, they cleared the table and opened their Bibles. " Let's open to the Book of John, the first chapter and the first three verses. Would you like to read it, Ella?"

"Let's let Dorothy read it and then we can discuss it. OK?"

"Alright, Dorothy, go ahead and read it."

"In the beginning," she read, "was the Word, and the Word was with God, and the Word was God. "

"Let's stop there for a few minutes" Howard interrupted. Do you notice anything peculiar about this sentence so far?" he asked.

"Well, for one thing Word is capitalized and it does it three times so it seems to me that God is trying to tell us something special about it," said Ella.

"Right!" said Howard delightedly. "What does it mean to you?"

"Well, I think Word is a person. Because the Bible says he was there in the beginning, that he was with God and that the Word was God. In other words he IS God!

"Excellent!" Now read on Dorothy and see if we can find out anything else about this person."

"The same was in the beginning with God. "

"Hmm. So Jesus didn't just come to earth in the form of a baby. He was always there from the very beginning. He IS the Word, he IS God, He was there at the Creation.

And something else happened that he was in on. Let's see if we can find out what that was."

Dorothy continued to read. "All things were made by Him and without him was not anything made that was made!"

"Wow! What do you get out of that?" Howard asked.

"That He was the creator! It says that nothing was made without him. And without him was not anything made that was made! I don't think I ever heard it this way before." Ella responded.

"I didn't either. That's why it shook me so hard. Ella, I think God has a special work for us to do and that this is just the beginning."

"I'm beginning to see why you got so excited about all this. " replied Ella. "You'll have to teach me and Dorothy, too, how to read and understand the Word."

"The best one to teach us is the Holy Spirit. He'll do that as we come to Jesus and read his Word. Shall we pray, now?" Howard asked.

They all knelt before the sofa and Howard lead in prayer. "Dear Jesus: You know this is our first attempt at family worship. We may stumble from time to time but we are in earnest and we love you so very much. Please open our understanding that we may know the truth so we don't lead others in the wrong ways. Give us many souls for our hire. Make us a blessing wherever we go. Bless Ella and Dorothy as they learn to lean on you. In your precious and Holy name we ask it. Amen"

Dorothy: "May I go next, Daddy?"

"Certainly."

Hesitantly at first, then becoming bolder as she found her way, Dorothy began to pray. "Father, I thank you for my new Daddy you have sent home to us. We pray you will give Tammy a special blessing for taking him to that meeting. Teach us your ways and help us to be obedient. I love you, Jesus. Amen"

Ella (weeping): 'Dear Jesus, it's a joy to hear our daughter pray like this. I'm ashamed that we waited this long to tell her about you but we're very thankful that Tammy had the nerve to take him to that meeting and that he found you there. Show us your will and help us to walk in it. In your precious name. Amen."

Howard sat, his head bowed, tears pouring down his cheeks., then reached over and clasped both of them to his chest. "If I never receive another gift in this life, I am so blessed tonight that I can't ask for anything more."

Ella: "Do you think it's too late to call Tammy? I'd like to thank her for taking you to that meeting."

"No, I don't think it's too late. I'm sure it would make her very happy."

"Good! I'll do that. What's her number?"

"It's in my briefcase. Just a minute and I'll get it."

He opened his briefcase and extracted the paper he had it on and handed it to her. She dialed the number and waited as the phone rang. Soon Tammy answered the phone " Hello?"

"Hello, Tammy. This is Ella. I wanted to thank you for taking Howard to that meeting. He's like a different person and just has talked and talked about all the people he met on this trip. We just had family worship and I asked him if it was too late to call you."

"Oh, Ella, thank *you* for calling me. I am so happy to hear from you. It seems like old times. Did you know the Lord before?"

"Not really. We went to church but it was more like a club where you met your friends but I never felt about the Lord like this before. And to hear my daughter pray! That was like Heaven. I just had to call and tell you. Here's Dorothy. She's been bugging me to let her talk to you."

Dorothy "Hi, Tammy. I feel like I know you! Daddy says he invited you and Tina and your mother to come out for Christmas. I'm so excited about it, I can hardly wait."

Tammy replied, "We'll sure try to make it and next time I go up to see Tina I'll let her call you. That will make her happy, too".

Dorothy: "That will make me happy, also. I feel like we're going to be good friends. Here's Mom"

Ella: "I think we should sign off now, but I want to turn the phone over to Howard so he can say his thanks, too. Here he is.""

Howard: "Hi, Tammy. Well, as you've heard, I've made a full report to my family. We had family worship tonight for the very first time and it was a time of joy for us. I think I'll have to send a letter with all the other things that happened on the plane home, etc. Ella and Dorothy can add a line or two also. That will be less expensive than phone calls. Good night and God bless you."

"Thank you. Howard. You're a blessing to me and will be to a great many people for I believe God has his hand on you. Good-night!"

As Howard hung up the phone, he turned to Ella and Dorothy, his face shining with joy. "You know," he said. "Tomorrow is Sunday. Would you like to go to that church that I told you about?"

"O, yes," Dorothy cried, "can we Mama?"

"Yes, I think I'd like to go and see what it's like. I'm sure Daddy will be happy about that too."

"I sure will! And now that that's settled I guess we'd better call it a night so we can get up early in the morning. I feel we should go to Sunday School, as well as church."

Giving Dorothy a big hug, he said "See you in the morning about 7:30. Set your alarm clock!"

"Night Daddy and Mama. I love you." She ran up the stairs to her room.

Howard placed his arm around Ella and drew her close to him. "Mmm, I sure do love you," he murmured as he kissed her and drew her to the stairs and up to their room. I was so afraid you wouldn't understand. I'm so happy. I think neither of us were being what the Lord intended us to be,"

"Yes, I know I wasn't. How much we were missing before!"

"Things will be different now."

They had undressed as they talked and now Howard tucked her in and strode around to his side of the bed and crawled in beside her. She cuddled up to him and he kissed her again as they settled down to sleep in each other's arms.

CHAPTER EIGHT

The next morning Dorothy was up before her alarm rang so she hurried and took her shower before her Mama and Daddy arose. Hearing her in the shower, they, too, arose and waited for her to get out of the shower. While they waited, they talked of the new excitement in their lives. Even Ella, hearing the difference in her husband began to get excited about the possibilities that might lie ahead for them.

Soon Dorothy was finished with her shower and Ella went next so she could get breakfast as Howard showered.

As they gathered at the table, they surmised what the day might hold for them as they ventured into new waters in their new Christian experience.

"I can't wait to see this new church and meet the people and their pastor." Dorothy cried. It's so exciting."

"I'm pretty excited myself," Ella replied. "It's made such a difference in your Daddy I can scarcely believe it. I think I want what he's got!"

Howard winked back the tears, got out his handkerchief and wiped his eyes. "You don't know how happy that makes me. I guess we'd better finish our breakfast and get on our way. It won't hurt for us to be a little early. I don't want to miss one minute of the service."

"I'll be ready as soon as I put on my dress and some make-up. Dorothy, will you rid up the table and put the dishes in the dishwasher?" Ella replied."

"I sure will," Dorothy answered. Soon Ella came downstairs and the three of them went to the garage and climbed into the car. "Oops, said Howard, "do you have your Bibles? I forgot mine." They held up their Bibles for him to see. "Be back in a minute." He cried as he hurried to grab the precious book he was learning to love and rely on so much.

It was at least a thirty-minute drive to the church they planned on attending. As they neared the parking lot, they were amazed at the line of cars waiting to enter and park. The parking lot was already nearly full. Evidently people came early to be sure of finding a parking place. The church itself was huge holding at least two thousand people

"My word!" Ella murmured. "What a crowd and what a beautiful building!"

The parking attendant flagged them to an available location and Howard pulled in, then they all climbed out of the car and headed for the entrance. The man Howard had met on the plane was standing at the door welcoming people as they entered. "Good morning, Howard" he said as they approached. "I take it this is your wife and daughter that you mentioned on the plane."

"Yes, this is my wife, Ella, and our daughter, Dorothy. They are very excited about coming to worship here."

"We're very happy to have you. I'll have one of the ushers show you around and introduce you. Try to sit near the front if you can. We try to pay special attention to people who attend for the first time."

"Thank you," Howard replied. "I guess I'd better leave that to the usher,"

"Okay, I'll talk to you later." He signaled to an usher to come and escort them up the aisle and find a seat for them.

It was another fifteen minutes before the service began, then the people stood and began to clap their hands in time to the music. The young man who played the keyboard was also the song director. As he sang, the people chimed in and began to sing as they continued to clap their hands. Dorothy was thrilled and entered right in. At first, Ella hung back as it was new and strange to her. Howard, having had a taste at the small meeting he had attended, fit right in. What a blessed service it was as they lifted their hands in praise to the King of Kings! For a good half-hour the congregation, together with the choir, continued to sing praises as one song after another poured forth their adoration to Him.

Then one of the Associate Pastors came up to lead the people in prayer and to offer prayer for any who needed healing or who, like Howard had, raised their hands to indicate their need of a Savior. Many of the members came up to help in this part of the service as they offered a shoulder to lean on, a heart-felt prayer for the salvation of some and healing for others. There was much rejoicing for the harvest of souls that was being brought in that morning.

Dorothy and Ella also joined those who came forward to accept Jesus as their Savior. As members of the congregation surrounded them and made them welcome with hugs of greeting, they began to feel a oneness and a belonging they had never felt before. Soon the congregation filed back to their seats and the Pastor rose to give the message.

"The message this morning is from the book of John, chapter 1 beginning at verse 6 through 12. 'There was a man sent from God, whose name was John. The same came for a witness, to bear witness of the Light, that all men through him might believe. He was not that Light, but was sent to bear witness of that Light. That was the true Light, which lighteth every man that cometh into the world. He was in the world, and the world was made by him, and the world knew him not. He came unto his own, and his own received him not', BUT as many as received, to them gave he power to become the sons of God, even to them which believe on his name." I say to all you that came forward this morning to accept Jesus as your Savior, that you were born again this morning, not of blood, nor of the will of the flesh, nor of the will of man, but of God!

"As you go forth today, be as a shining light to all you meet. Don't be timid. Not everyone to whom you speak the word will respond in kind. Not everyone will believe but see that you live as if their lives depended on your testimony by your actions and your speech. God will give you many souls if you do this. Read his Word daily and talk to Him. He will strengthen you. May God bless you and keep you until we meet again."

The strains of 'God be with you till we meet again poured forth from the orchestra as the people filed out. Many spoke to Howard and Ella and Dorothy welcoming them to their midst.

As they went out to their car, they were silent as they pondered the Pastor's words and the scene they had participated in that morning. Howard's heart was full to overflowing as he thanked God for saving Dorothy and Ella, too.

"Would you like to go to a restaurant for dinner?" he asked.

"That would be nice.' Ella responded.

"Oh, yes!" Dorothy agreed.

"Okay. There's a nice restaurant about half a mile from here. Let's try that."

Evidently many of the people from the church had also decided to eat there for the parking lot was full and many of the people they had met at church welcomed them. Finding a table near the group they sat down but some of the church members asked the waitress if they could put the tables together so they could all eat together, which she gladly did. Soon there was a jolly conversation going as they waited for their dinners to come. Ella was drawn into the group of women and soon became a part of their activities. Dorothy, of course, became involved with the younger ones in the group. When their dinners arrived one of the men asked Howard if he would ask the blessing. He was happy to oblige and as they all bowed their heads, he prayed, "Father, we come together today to thank you for the beautiful service this morning and for all those who accepted Jesus as their Savior. We also thank you for all those you healed. We thank you for the fellowship of these believers and for this food which you have blessed. We praise and thank you, in Jesus' name."

As people finished their dinners, they began to disperse one by one, calling 'Goodbye to all including Howard and his family. Then they, too, wended their way home.

CHAPTER NINE

Next morning, Howard hurried to his pharmacy, anxious to see how the business had progressed while he was gone. Tom was already there before him and Howard greeted him with a hug around his shoulder.

"Well," Tom asked, "how was your trip?"

"It was fabulous. Do you remember a girl named Tammy in high school?"

"Not really," Tom replied. "Why?"

"Well, she's living in New York now and I met her there. She was smiling at me and I could see her reflection in the window where I was looking at a display of some of the items I wanted to get for the store. Finally I turned around and said, "Should I know you?" She laughed and said, "Yes, I was two years behind you in High school.. I had a crush on you because you were the fullback for the football team. I'm Tammy Waring. Then I remembered that she wore braces on her teeth and pigtails in her hair. She sure looks different now. Anyway, I took her to dinner and wanted to take her to a movie afterwards but she said 'no' she had someplace else she'd like to go to so, what could I do? I went along. Anyway, it was a religious meeting she took me to and I gave my heart to the Lord that night. I told Ella and Dorothy about it and they have given their hearts to the Lord, too. Think you might like to go to church with us.? You might like it, too."

"Nah, I don't go in for that kind of stuff. I got other things to do."

"Sorry to hear you say that! Well, we'll just continue to pray for you. After all, you're my partner and one of my best friends. Talk to you later."

Meanwhile, Iris, Ella's neighbor had dropped in for a chat and a cup of coffee. "How was Howard's trip?" she asked.

"Iris, you wouldn't believe the change in that man. It's just like I got a new husband."

"Why? What happened to him?"

"Well, a girl that we both knew in high school took him to a meeting where she was leading the singing. As a result he gave his heart to the Lord. Then he met this man on the plane who is the pastor of a large church in Phoenix. We went there yesterday morning. It's so different from the church we had been going to. Maybe you can go with us sometime. Would you like to?"

"I don't really know. I'll have to ask George and see what he says. Neither of us really enjoy that sort of thing. But I'll ask him anyway."

Disappointed because her first attempt at winning a soul for Jesus didn't take root right away, Ella wisely turned the talk to other things. " Howard brought home a lot of nice things for Dorothy and me. He's going to take both of us the next time he goes and he's invited Tammy and her daughter and her mother to come here for a vacation for Christmas week so you'll get to meet them. I'll probably have a big Christmas Party. That's something you and George will just *have* to come to!"

"Of course, we will. You'll probably need a lot of help, too. That's something I can do."

"You know, it's only about six weeks from now. That time will go awfully fast!" remarked Ella. "I'll have to start getting invitations out and planning meals and everything else right away."

"Well, count me in. I'll be right next door and can help at a moment's notice."

"Thank you, Iris. I'll sure count on that and take you up on it."

CHAPTER TEN

As the days wore on, both Howard and Ella tried to witness to other people but found that they needed some training so they enrolled in a class on Thursday nights that provided special training for witnessing. Dorothy wanted to be involved also, so she, too, joined that group. Although they hoped the Senior Pastor would be doing the training, an associate pastor had been assigned to teach it. He seemed to be especially led of the Lord for this work, however, and they all began to grow spiritually as they learned.

Although Howard's partner still resisted any advances Howard made, he was nevertheless making great strides with some of his customers as they came in to look at the things he had purchased for Christmas giving in New York. He used every opportunity to introduce his Lord to the people who came to buy. Santa Claus didn't have a place in his store! As far as he was concerned, his business belonged to the Lord and he gave Him all the glory.

Ella, too, had joined a ladies' group at the church and she began, little by little, to tell them of Tammy and how she had been instrumental in leading Howard to the Lord. She told them about the coming visit at Christmas-time and invited them to join in the festivities to welcome them. Many offered to make their favorite goodies for the occasion. Rather than the occasion becoming a burden, Ella began to look forward to it with anticipation.

Although Iris still didn't make any move to attend worship services on Sunday, she did accompany Ella to a couple of the ladies' meetings and as she began to become acquainted with many of the women, she, too, became excited about the coming visit and began to make suggestions to Ella about some of the things they could do to make the visit special.

One night as Howard was attending the training class, the Sr. Pastor came and sat in on the class. He was amazed at the wisdom that Howard had acquired. It had to be from the Holy Spirit! As Howard related how the Holy Spirit had used John 1 to introduce him and Ella and Dorothy to Jesus and showed them how Jesus himself was the Word and that He *was God himself. That He was there in the beginning and that everything that was made was also made by Him.*

Again in John 14: 8-14 Philip said to Jesus: Show us the Father. Jesus replied, "Have I been so long with you, and yet hast thou not known me, Philip? He that hath <u>seen</u> me, hath seen the Father, and how sayest thou then, show us the Father? Believest thou not that I am in the Father, and the Father in me? The words that I speak unto you, I speak not of myself; but the Father that dwelleth in me, he doeth the works! Believe me that I am in the Father and the Father in me: or else believe me for the very works' sake.

Verily I say unto you, He that believeth on me, the works that I do shall he do also, and greater works than these shall he do also, because I go unto my Father and whatsoever ye ask in my name, that will I do that the Father may be glorified in the Son. If ye shall ask anything in my name, I will do it.

Only believe! What a truth that is! If only people could comprehend it and embrace that truth and practice it in their lives what a different world this would be.

Not wanting to intervene in the teaching that was taking place, the Sr. Pastor waited until after the class was dismissed to speak to Howard. "I am amazed at your comprehension of these truths. God is surely leading you into some avenue of service to Him. May God bless you and use you mightily."

"Thank you," Howard replied. "He has created a great hunger in me to publish these truths in any way that I can."

"Just keep it up! You're doing great and I believe God has a plan for your life and will use you mightily."

As Howard turned to go home, his heart swelled with gladness that the Lord whom he had come to love so dearly might use him in ways that he could not yet imagine.

CHAPTER ELEVEN

When Howard got home one evening, he said to Ella, "Darling, I want to study for awhile. Will you call me when dinner is ready? I'll be in my den. OK?"

"Of course, dear. I'll call you when dinner is ready."

He went into his den and got on his knees before his Lord, "Dear Jesus," he prayed. "I feel a special call of some kind on my life but I am at a loss to know what your will is concerning me. Will you please enlighten me so that I don't waste time doing things that are not profitable for you.? Time is so precious for many souls who might be thrust into eternity without you if Satan has his way. As I read your word tonight,, will you cause it to become a spotlight before me that I might know your will for me. I love you, Lord. Amen." Howard rose from his knees and took his Bible over to his easy chair. Opening his Bible to the Book of John, he went back to the beginning of the book where he had first read that Jesus was present in the Beginning before the world was made.

John, the Baptist, speaks of himself in John 1:6 "There was a man sent from God, whose name was John. The same came for a witness, to bear witness of the Light, that all men through him might believe. He was not that Light, but *was sent* to bear witness of that Light. That was the true Light, which lighteth every man that cometh into the world. He was in the world, and the world was made by him and the world knew him not. He came unto his own, and his own received him not! But as many as received him, to them gave he power to become the sons of God even to them that believe on his name.

Howard dropped to his knees, tears blurring his vision as he remembered the words he had just read. " Dear Jesus, I thank you for these words for I *have received you*, and you said you will give those who receive you power to become the sons of God even to them who believe on your name. How blessed we are!. Please use me, and Ella and Dorothy also. Show us the way you'd have us to go.. In your own precious name, I ask it."

He had just said those words when Ella called to tell him dinner was ready. Wiping the tears from his eyes, he got to his feet and went downstairs to dinner.

"Mmm. Something sure smells good. What are we having tonight?"

"Chicken tenders with garden vegetables in sauce, a dish of spinach with vinegar, bacon bits and hard-boiled eggs sliced over it."

"No dessert?" he cried.

"How about pumpkin pie with whipped cream?" Ella laughed.

"You were teasing me, weren't you?" he laughed. "Well, let's ask the blessing so we can dig in to this delicious meal.. 'Father, we bow our heads in thanksgiving for all your bountiful blessings. Thank you for this food which you have provided for us through the loving hands of a faithful wife. And for our obedient daughter who also loves you so much. No man could be more blessed. Keep us close to you, in the name of your precious Son, Jesus. Amen"

"You know, honey," Ella said as she passed the food.

"I was thinking today that we ought to make arrangements to get the airline tickets for Tammy and her mother and daughter before it gets too close to the holidays. Tickets might be hard to come by if we wait too close to the holidays. You can do that right on the internet, can't you?"

"Yes, I can but I think I'd better call Tammy first and see what days she will have free to come. I don't believe her mother works and Tina's school should be out for the holidays so it will all depend on when Tammy can get free from her job.. I'll call her right after dinner before we have family worship. "

Tammy and the Pharmacist

"I think that's a good idea." Ella replied. " Have you heard anything from the couple whose wife you met on the plane? We ought to have them over at least once before Tammy comes."

"No, I've been so busy I haven't had time to call them. Guess I'd better do that, too. Will it be all right if we have our dessert after 'family worship'?

"Sure. This is Friday night and Dorothy won't have to get up early tomorrow."

"Right. I'll call Tammy from the living room. Do you want to speak to her?"

"Not unless she asks for me. I don't want to take time that we will need to make those reservations.."

"Okay, I'll call her now."

Lifting the phone, Howard dialed Tammy's number. The phone rang a few times and he began to think she wasn't at home, then she lifted the receiver and said" Hello/"

"Tammy, it's Howard. I'm sorry I haven't called sooner but we've been very busy taking special classes at the church where we worship now."

"That's all right. Is everything else all right?"

"Yes, but I wanted to find out what day you will be able to leave from your job so I can get the airline tickets ordered. Do you know yet?"

"Not really, Howard. We might not be able to come. My job has been cancelled and I don't think there will be another opening here. I don't know what to do!"

"Oh, no! Look, you just have to come. Maybe you can find a job here. Motorola is hiring. I'm sure, with your background, you could get a good job there. Have you already been laid off?"

"Yes. Just today. That's why I was so long in answering the phone. I've been pretty upset."

"I don't wonder at that. Is your rent paid for the month? Do you have any money to live on until you can get here?"

"Yes, my rent is paid until the first, and I have enough money for a few days groceries."

"That relieves my mind a little bit. Just a minute, I want you to talk to Ella. It was her idea for me to call and get tickets before it was too late because of the holidays. Hold on while I get her."

"Ella," he called. "Will you come and talk to Tammy? She's lost her job and I'm trying to persuade her to come anyway and try to get a job at Motorola."

"Oh, my." Ella cried as she took the phone. "Tammy?

You have to come out and let us help you. Don't worry about lodging or anything else. I believe this is of the Lord.

If it wasn't for you, we wouldn't be having this beautiful relationship with him now. Will you come and bring your Mom and Tina, too. We'll manage just fine. OK?"

"All right. Whenever Howard can get the tickets. I'll call Mom and tell her."

"Fine. Here's Howard."

Howard took the phone, "Tammy? I'll call the airlines and see what I can find. Then I'll call you back. Meanwhile, Ella says you were going to call your mother. That'll give me time to get on the Internet and see what I can find for you."

"OK. I'll wait for your call."

CHAPTER TWELVE

Tammy dialed the phone again to call her mother.

"Hello?'" her mother answered.

"Mom, it's Tammy."

"Tammy! Is something the matter? You sound like you've been crying."

"Yes, Mom, I have been. I have some bad news and some good news. Today, I was laid off permanently from my job. The good news is that Howard and Ella just called. They were getting ready to get the airline tickets and when I told them about my job, they insisted that I come out right away and they think I can get a good job at Motorola. They want you and Tina to come, too."

"Oh, Tammy, I can't do that! You know I own this house. I'd have to sell it if I moved out there. I have all my friends and my church here. But you and Tina go ahead anyway. I believe like Ella says that this is of the Lord. "I'll be just fine and I can come out for a visit when you get settled. OK?"

"OK, Mom. I believe that is a good idea. I just hate to leave you behind. Is Tina still awake? I'd like to talk to her a minute, if she is."

"Yes, she's right here waiting." She handed Tina the phone.

"Hi, Mom. I thought that was you. Are we going out to Dorothy's house right away?"

"Yes. Howard is on the phone out there trying to make airline reservations right now. As soon as I know, I'll call back and let you know. You'll need to get all your clothes and everything packed."

"Oh, Mom, I'm so excited. It will be wonderful to be where you are for a change. I love Grandma but I sometimes feel like I'm a burden on her, too. Call me soon. I love you"

"Okay, I love you, too! Bye for now."

CHAPTER THIRTEEN

Tammy had no more than hung up the phone when it rang. "Hello?"

"Tammy, it's Howard. I was able to get tickets for next Wednesday morning at 7 A.M. your time. Is that too soon?"

"No, it's not too soon but you will have to cancel the ticket for Mom. She says she would have to sell her house and she doesn't feel ready to do that but she says she'll come out and visit when we are all settled later on."

"That will be no problem. I'll do that when I call back to confirm your reservation. Since you don't have a computer, I'll have them fax your tickets to you and I will also get a copy on my computer so I'll know when to expect you."

"Oh, Howard, I don't know how to thank you. But I'm sure the Lord will bless you greatly! This will give me time to go up and get Tina and her luggage over the weekend and to get my luggage packed, too. I rented this place furnished so I won't need to worry about things like that."

"Sounds like we have a plan! Dorothy is in ecstasy! She's so thrilled that you're both coming. Ella is, too."

"And I am thrilled, too, now that I'm used to the idea.
It's almost like I'm coming home!"

"We want you to feel that way. God bless and keep you. Call collect if you need to. We'll accept the charges.'Bye now."

CHAPTER FOURTEEN

The next morning, which was Saturday, Tammy arose early and after eating a bowl of oatmeal, she got her luggage together and started out for her mother's hone. She had called her mother earlier to let her know she was on her way so that Tina could start getting her clothes and other accessories together for the trip back. She knew she didn't have much time to waste if she would have everything ready when the plane they were to catch was ready for them on Wednesday morning. She would have to let her friends at work know she was leaving, too, as well as the group she had been worshipping with.

She had made good time and found that by eleven o'clock she was almost there. She had to stop for gasoline so she decided to got to the bathroom and also get a bite to eat as she had eaten so early. Then she got back on the road again. It had started to snow a little bit and was getting colder as she got farther north. "I think I'm going to like Phoenix," she said to herself. "It will be much warmer there. I don't really care for snow and ice. I wish Mom didn't have to live way up here but it's where her heart is. Some day maybe she'll change her mind and come out to stay with us. Dear Father, I'm so glad you worked all this out for us. I'm sure it was your doing! Thank you for all you do for me. Bless Howard, Ella and Dorothy. Thank you again for their wonderful friendship. Please have a job ready for me. I don't want to be a burden on these dear friends. In Jesus precious name I ask it. Amen."

CHAPTER FIFTEEN

It was almost one o'clock when Tammy turned into the driveway at her mother's home. Tina was watching for her and came running out to the car to welcome her. "Hi! Mom. I'm so glad to see you."

"I'm glad to see you, too," Tammy replied, "but you'd better get back in the house. You don't even have a sweater on. You don't want to catch pneumonia, do you?"

"I'm sorry, Mom. I'm just so excited that I just couldn't wait for you to come in."

"Well, let's both get in there right now. I'll get my luggage later." She got out of the car, wrapped her arms around Tina and both ran for the house. Tammy's Mom was waiting at the door and ushered them in.

"Oh, Mom, Everything has happened so fast I can scarcely take it all in but Howard and Ella are being so wonderful. It's like a fairy tale coming true! I was so discouraged last night and now here I am getting ready to fly to Arizona! It's really almost like going home. Life sure takes some funny turns sometimes, doesn't it?"

"Yes, it does! But you have to remember that you have a powerful ally in the Lord Jesus and he knows just when to make things happen."

"Oh, how well I know that! I've been wanting to find some way to have Tina with me and here Jesus had it all planned out when I didn't even know it."

"Yes, I'm going to miss having her with me but she needs to be with you and she needs friends her own age, too. I understand you'll be going to a wonderful church out there!"

"Yes, Jesus has everything all planned out. All we have to do is follow his leading."

"Well, let's get your luggage in. Tina has most of her things already packed. Did you have any lunch?"

"Yes, I stopped about eleven o'clock to get gas so I got some lunch there. I didn't want to stop again."

"Well, I have something cooking in the Slow Cooker so we can eat whenever you get hungry. Maybe you need to take a nap. You must have gotten up pretty early."

"Yes, I did, but I was too excited to sleep anyway. I think I'll just go to bed early. OK?"

'Yes, we got up early, too, so we'll probably feel like going to bed early, also"

"I sure hope this snow lets up before morning. I hate to drive in the snow."

"Well, Jesus had everything else planned out. He can take care of a little snow. Go get your bags so you can unpack what you need. Are you going to be able to stay over tomorrow?"

'"Not really, Mom. I have everything to pack yet at the apartment so I'll need every spare minute I can get. Our plane leaves early Wednesday morning. I also need time to let some of my friends know what has happened and where I'll be."

"I understand. I'll miss you terribly but I think this is for the best."

Tammy ran out to her car to get her luggage and lock her car up. Then took her things up to Tina's room where she would sleep that night. By then dinner was ready and they decided to eat then so they could make an early night of it.

CHAPTER SIXTEEN

Tammy arose at 6 A.M. the next morning and woke Tina up so they could get an early start. Meanwhile, her mother, hearing them up went down to fix a good hearty breakfast of bacon, eggs and hot biscuits so they wouldn't get hungry on the road. It had quit snowing during the night for which they were glad.

As they sat down to the table, Tammy's Mom bowed her head and gave thanks to the Savior who was so bountifully caring for all of them. Not only did she thank him for the food, but for the cessation of the snow which had worried them. Surely they were secure in his care!

Tammy moved to help rid up the dishes but her Mom said, "No, you and Tina need to be on your way. I can do these and still get ready for church on time."

"I wish we could stay and go to church with you but I guess we'll just have to listen on the car radio. There was a real good Christian station on when I was coming up here."

So saying, they shrugged into their coats, grabbed their luggage and carried it out to the car. Not bothering to put it in the trunk, they just piled it into the back seat. Tammy and Tina hugged her mother who had come out to bid them goodbye, each of them shedding a few tears. Then tearing them selves away, they climbed in to the car and drove away.

CHAPTER SEVENTEEN

Tammy drove steadily for about four hours when she noticed the gas gauge was getting pretty low. "I guess we'd better stop at the next gas station and get gas," she said to Tina.

"Yes, I need to go to the bathroom, too, Mom. Do you suppose we could get a hamburger or something? I'm kind of hungry, too."

"Yes, we can do that. It's almost noon, anyway. We should be home by three o'clock at the latest. There's a sign for a gas station and I believe there's a restaurant right next to it. We'll stop there."

Pulling in to the nearest pump Tammy waited for the service man to come help her. She turned to Tina. "Can you wait until we pull up to the restaurant to go to the bathroom? This place doesn't look too clean."

"Yes, Mom. I can wait. I'm glad we found a place tho'. I am getting pretty hungry. I'll sure be glad when we get to your apartment."

"Me, too," Tammy replied. "All this driving is using up my energy. It will be nice to fly."

"What are you going to do with your car, Mom? You can't take it out on the plane."

"Of course I can't! But I think Robert will try to sell it for me and send me the money. I'll have to buy another one when I get a job out there. I'm just not going to let a thing worry me, though. I'll just trust the Lord. He's taken care of everything so far."

"He sure has, Mom. I'm so glad we know Him.. I'd trust Him with anything."

As the station attendant finished servicing their car, Tammy paid him and drove over to the restaurant and parked in front of it. They locked the car and went inside. Tina hurried to the rest room while Tammy found a table and settled in until Tina returned so she could take her turn. "You order," she said to Tina as she left to go to the rest room.

The waitress approached the table and asked Tina if she was ready to order.

"Yes, Tina replied. "We'd like two hamburgers with everything on them and two strawberry milkshakes."

She had barely finished ordering when Tammy returned. " I see you've already ordered." Tammy noted.

"Well, Tina replied, " I pretty well know what you like and I like the same thing so I thought I'd just order to save time. Besides, I was getting awfully hungry."

Tammy laughed, " I thought there was a bit of 'method in your madness' as the old saying goes."

"Well, "Tina said defensively, " I was also thinking of you having to drive all this way. Sure wish I was old enough to drive."

"Don't rush it! You'll get old enough before you know it."

"Oh, Mom, I'm so happy to be with you again. I love Grandma but it's just not the same as being with your own mother."

"Yes, I realize that but do you realize she's *my mother* and we, too, have a relationship that it's hard to break away from.."

"Golly, Mom, I never thought about that! I'm sorry. Maybe she can come out later to at least visit with us."

"Yes. She might even come out to spend the winter months with us. It's so cold here and beautiful out there."

"Are we almost there yet? I'm beginning to get kinda tired."

"Yes. We should be there within an hour at the most."

" Do you have to let Howard know when you get home?"

"Yes, I think I should and he will be able to let me know what flight we'll be on and what time it leaves."

Tina slid down in her seat to get into a more comfortable position. Soon she was fast asleep. Tammy drove on and soon turned into the street where she lived. Pulling into the driveway, she noticed a car at the curb. "I wonder who that is," she whispered to herself.

Turning to wake Tina, she said," Tina, wake up. We're home and somebody is out front waiting for me."

Tina roused herself and turned to Tammy. "Do you know who it is?"

"Not yet," Tammy answered. "Someone's getting out of the car now and coming this way. —-Oh!, it's Robert Warren from our worship group. He's just the person I wanted to see. C'mon, we'll let him in and maybe he'll help us unload some of this luggage."

"Where have you been? Robert inquired. "We've been worried sick about you."

"C'mon in and I'll tell you all about it."

"OK but it had better be good!" he teased.

"Well, it's sad in a way, and completely wonderful in another. First, I lost my job. It wasn't anything I did or didn't do. Macy's just turned the whole audit department over to an auditing firm and there just wasn't any more job for me. Well, I was pretty down. I didn't know what I was going to do. Do you remember the man you led to the Lord that night when I brought him to our meeting? Well, he and his wife had invited us to come out for Christmas for a vacation. He called me Friday night to see what day we could come and when he heard I had lost my job, nothing would do but he wanted us to come out right away and see if I could get a job out there with Motorola. Anyway, our plane leaves Wednesday morning for Phoenix, Arizona and I had to go up to my mother's to get my daughter and bring her back with me. We just got back when we pulled in."

"Whew! What a story! You won't be living here anymore?"

"No, I'm afraid not. They insisted we stay with them until I got a job and got situated. Howard has a daughter the same age as Tina, and his wife and I knew each other in High School. They are both involved in a special ministry and going to a wonderful church with over 2,000 people in Phoenix. It's just like God had everything all worked out ahead of time!"

"Is there anything I can do to help?"

"Yes, there is one thing. If I give you the title for my car can you get it sold for me and send me part of the money? I'll just need enough to get groceries, etc. until I get a pay check and a place to live?"

"Sure, I will. And I'll get as good a price as I can and send you the whole thing. I don't want a thing for helping out a very good friend."

"I knew I could count on you. It's just like God had you sitting there waiting for me. Everything has been going that way. It's almost unbelievable but it's true!"

"That's the way our Lord is and I'm sorry to see you go but I'm happy for you also. I know God will send us someone to take your place but we sure will miss you."

"Thank you. Can you come sometime tomorrow to get the papers for the car transferred to you so you can sell it?"

"Yes. It'll have to be around 3:30 as I have another errand to do but I will be here. I'll also take you to the airport and help you with your luggage. Do you know what time your plane leaves yet?"

"No, I have to call Howard now and find that out. Can you stay while I call him? He might want to talk to you, too."

"Yes, I'd love to talk to him. You go right ahead and call him. I'll wait."

"OK. " She lifted the phone and began dialing the number.

Howard answered the phone. "Hello"

"Howard, it's Tammy. We just got home and Robert, the one who led you to the Lord was here and he's helping us on this end. Would you like to talk to him?"

"I sure would!"

"Hello, Howard. I've been hearing some pretty wonderful things about you. "

"Well, I think I owe it all to you, Robert. You sure changed my life around."

"I was just doing the Lord's will. He had it all planned out, even down to having Tammy find you like she did."

"I feel very humble when I think of how much he cared about me to go to such lengths to see me saved!"

"Ah, but he had a plan for your life! You have no idea yet what he is going to do through you. I just hope you'll be able to make others see the possibilities and the joy there is in serving Jesus."

"I'll sure try! Now I need to talk again to Tammy for a few minutes. Okay?

"Right. Here she is." He handed the phone back to Tammy.
"Yes, Howard?"
"About the plane tickets. They have sent me a copy and will be faxing yours to you tomorrow. So you should have them in plenty of time. The airline will also have a copy of your tickets. So don't worry about a thing."

"Okay. Robert is going to see us to the airport and he is going to sell my car and send me the money so everything seems to be working out okay. I'll talk to you or Ella tomorrow night. Good-night and God bless you."

"I've gotta run, too." Robert said. See you tomorrow afternoon. 'Night."

"Good-night, Robert! And please convey my apologies to the rest or our group. I wish I had time for one more meeting but I don't so you'll have to do it for me. I'll see you tomorrow. Thanks again for all your help." Tammy closed the door after him and locked it. Then turning out the lights, she and Tina went into the bedroom to get what they hoped to be a 'good night's rest'.

CHAPTER EIGHTEEN

Having gone to bed so early, Monday morning found them wide awake at six AM. Tammy yawned and then turned to see if Tina was awake yet and, of course, she was! They both hopped out of bed and hurried to use the bathroom and get dressed. They were so excited. Just one more day and they would be on their way to an entirely new life. This day promised to be full, though. Robert would be there in the afternoon to take care of the transfer of her car and the tickets should either be in the mail or faxed by telephone. Since she didn't have a computer, she imagined it would have to be by mail or telegram. However they came, Tammy knew that Howard would know how to do it right."

Tina, of course, was so excited she didn't know where to start so Tammy got a few jobs for her to do. She dragged out a huge trunk and they both packed sheets, blankets and towels, etc. in it.. Tammy set Tina to washing any soiled clothing they had while she packed heavy articles in the trunk. By the time Robert was due they had everything pretty well under control.

Robert rang the doorbell and Tina ran to let him in. "We'll have to go right away," he said,"as the court house closes at four-thirty. Are you ready to go now?"

"Yes, we're ready" Tammy replied. "I have all the papers, too, so I don't think there'll be any problem."

"OK, let's go then."

They finished just as the courthouse was ready to close. Robert turned to Tammy," How about you and Tina having dinner with me?" he asked.

Tammy and the Pharmacist

"Oh, you're doing so much for us already. We can eat when we get home."

"Yes, but since I'm a bachelor, I'd enjoy having two pretty ladies to eat dinner with!"

Tammy laughed. "Since you put it that way, how can we say 'No'?"

Robert helped them in the car, then drove away to a nice restaurant he knew of.

Tammy didn't realize just how hungry she was but Tina was always hungry so he had two hungry ladies on his hands. They had forgotten to eat lunch, they were so busy.

When Robert drove up to a snazzy restaurant, they were ready for anything. A hamburger would have been a delight to them but this was lush! He helped them out of the car and took one of them on each arm. Tammy giggled like a schoolgirl. "I haven't had such fun in a long time." she said.

"That's how I was hoping to make you feel'" Robert replied as he led them to a table. The waitress approached as they seated themselves. "Can I take you order?"

"May we have a look at the menu first, please," he asked.

"Certainly. Would you like me to come back in a few minutes?"

"If you would, please." "Now, what would you girls like?"

"Why don't you just order for us?" Tammy suggested.

"You're welcome to order anything you like. How about you, Tina?

"I'd just like anything that's got chicken in it." She responded.

"I guess that goes for me, too." Tammy said.

"Then that's what we'll have." Robert retorted. "How about a salad, a vegetable and mashed potatoes?"

"Sounds good to me, Tammy and Tina said in one breath. They all laughed and Robert signaled the waitress that they were ready.

After the waitress had taken their order, they sat and talked while they waited for their dinner. Tammy was becoming more relaxed as the evening wore on. It seemed the strain and stress of the last few days had just melted away.

When their dinner came, Robert bowed his head to give thanks to their Lord.

As they ate, Robert asked questions about where they were going and what their plans were. Tammy and Tina told him what little they knew about the place they were going to. Tina had never been there but Tammy grew up there so it was more familiar to her. She said it was like going back home but she would miss her mother being there.

Their waitress came back to see if they wanted some dessert. Tammy said she was stuffed but Tina wanted a dish of ice cream and Robert said he would have pie ala mode.

"Ooh, that sounds wonderful. Can I change my order?"

Robert laughed, "You sure can!" "OK "he said to the waitress. She smiled and went away to get the order.

As they finished their dinner, Tammy thanked Robert for the lovely evening and the sumptuous dinner he had treated them to. Soon they were back in the car and on their way to their apartment. Although Tammy was quite tired, she politely asked Robert if he'd like to come in. He responded with a shake of his head. "I think it's about time for me to hit the hay, too." He said. "I'll see you tomorrow. If I'm able to sell the car then, you'll be able to take the money with you."

"That's awfully nice of you but don't you have work to do and everything? We don't have to have the money right away."

"Well, you see, I'm a car salesman and I can take some time off when I need to. It's not a nine to five job like some people have. I like that. It also leaves me some free time when I want to minister to someone."

"Was that what you were doing tonight, ministering?

He laughed, "Not really. I was pleasing my self with two very lovely ladies that I might not see again, once they leave here."

"Maybe sometime you'll get out to Phoenix and can look us up."

"That's a very strong possibility. I just might do that."

"Be sure you give us your address and phone number so we can keep in touch. Do you have a computer?'

"Why, yes I do. Do you?"

"No, I don't yet but I do want to get one. I used one in my job at Macy's but I couldn't afford one at home."

"Well, I'll see that you get my e-mail address, also.. Now I know you're tired and so am I. I'll see you tomorrow. Good-night."

CHAPTER NINETEEN

It was around ten o'clock Tuesday morning when Robert came to get her car. Leaving his car at the apartment, he drove hers to the used car lot where he intended to try to sell it. Tammy and Tina busied themselves with the rest of their packing. Knowing she wouldn't be able to take too much luggage on the plane, she decided to pack a large trunk with pictures and keepsakes she couldn't make herself give up. She was sure Robert would have them shipped for her.

Fortunately, she only had a month-to-month lease so all she needed to do was call the owner and tell her she was moving and why. She was sure she would understand.

It was almost one o'clock when Robert came back in a taxi. He came up the hall waving a sheaf of bills at her.

"Oh, Robert," Tammy cried. "Don't tell me you sold the car already!"

"I sure did! Got a good price, too. Here, hold out your hands."

Tammy held out her hands and he began to count the bills into her hand – one hundred, two hundred, three hundred, four hundred, five hundred plus five hundred makes one thousand dollars!"

"Oh, Robert, did you really get that much for that old car?"

"Sure did."

"Ooh! I could hug you!"

"Be my guest. I haven't been hugged by a pretty lady. Tammy gave him a big hug, then asked if she could beg one more favor from him.

"Certainly. What would you like me to do?"

"Well, I know there are limits to what you can take on a plane so I wondered if you could take this trunk to the post office and have it shipped to Arizona for me?"

"Sure could! Is it ready to go now?"

"Yes." Tammy replied.

"Then there's no time like the present. Why don't I take it now and have it over with?"

"Did you have any lunch? Maybe we'd better have lunch first."

"I'm not really hungry and I have a customer coming at three-thirty so I need to get back to the sales room "

"How thoughtless of me!" Tammy cried. " I should have known you would have work to do. Please forgive me."

"There's no problem. I have plenty of time to get back to the sales room. This guy is already sold. It's just a matter of finalizing the sales contract. Don't worry your pretty head about it.. As I told you before, my time is my own and I will be able to take care of it for you. I'm just sorry, now that we've got to know each other that you're going to be so far away."

"I am, too, but we never know what God is going to do in our lives, do we?"

"I have to run, now. I'll see you around five A.M. tomorrow morning so be ready! You won't want to miss that plane. "'Bye for now."

CHAPTER TWENTY

The next morning, Tammy and Tina awoke early and, unable to sleep any more they decided to get up, have breakfast and double check to see that everything they needed had been packed.

They had a leisurely breakfast and after they had washed the dishes, Tammy remembered that she hadn't called her land-lady yet, even though her rent was paid to the end of the month, she owed her the courtesy of an advance notice

After they had washed up their dishes and put them away, she took up the phone and dialed her landlady's phone.

"Hello?" the landlady answered her ring.

"This is Tammy Waring, Mrs. Beavers. I'm sorry to tell you that I have to give up the apartment. I lost my job and and friends in Arizona have made arrangements for me to come out there and stay with them until I can get a job there. I'm sorry this is such short notice but I didn't know till Sunday that all this was going to happen. My rent is paid until the first of next month so you'll have time to get it rented again. "

"That's all right, Ms. Waring. You've been a very good tenant. When will your plane leave?"

"I think early Wednesday morning. I'm not sure about the time yet. I've got to call the friend who is getting the tickets for me and my daughter tonight. He's getting them over the internet and they should be faxed to me tomorrow. Where do you want me to leave the keys?"

"Could you leave them with your next door neighbor? She's my tenant, also. I know you'll need them to lock up when you leave.

I'm sure she'll be glad to take care of them for me. I'll call her to be sure. OK? I'll call you to let you know. God bless you where you're going."

"Thank you, Mrs. Beavers"

Tammy heaved a big sigh. "One more thing done. I sure will be glad when it's all done, won't you, Tina?"

"I sure will, Mom. I hope there's no problem with the tickets."

"Well, I'll call Howard this evening as soon as he's home from work and find out, especially if we don't get anything in the mail to confirm our reservations."

"Can't they fax them to the reservation desk at the airport. It seems I heard someone say they had that done for them."

"I think so but we'll ask Howard just to be sure."

"I guess we've got everything packed and all cleaned up here. I don't know what to do with myself with so much time on my hands."

"Could we watch television for a little while?"

"I don't know what's on. Do you like to read? I've got some good books you might enjoy. I thought I might take them on the plane. There's television on the plane, too, so you'll probably enjoy that."

"I guess I'll go check and see if we got any mail yet. Maybe the tickets have come."

"Can I come along? I get so bored just sitting around."

"OK, but stay with me. New York streets are not a safe place for a young girl. Tomorrow we'll be on our way. Then you won't be bored anymore." She opened the mailbox but there was just some junk mail. No tickets. They started back up the stairs when they heard the phone ringing. Tammy ran to pick it up before whoever was calling would hang up. Fortunately, it was the landlady.

"Ms. Waring," she said. "The lady in the next apartment said she'd be glad to keep the keys for me so when you leave just knock on her door and leave them with her. Have a good trip."

"Thank you," Tammy replied as she hung up. She turned to look for Tina but didn't see her. "Tina!" She called, "Where are you?" Running down the stairs, she looked wildly about. Then she saw her talking with a girl about her own age. She heaved a sigh of relief, then walked over to talk to the two of them. She noticed the other girl was smoking a cigarette. Rather than make an issue in front of the other girl, she tried diplomatically to get Tina to come back upstairs rather than make an issue of it. How she wished they had time to establish a relationship. "Lord," she prayed, " show me what to do. How can I witness to this young girl in a way that will make her want to follow you?"

"Would you like to come upstairs to the apartment and visit a little while? I could make some lemonade and I think we've got a few cookies left." If I can only get her name and address, she thought, I can leave it with Robert and he and the group I've been worshipping with could get in touch with her.

"Why, yes. I think I'd like that!" So the three of them climbed up the stairs and sat down in the living room.

"Do you live near here?" Tina asked.

"Yes, I live around the corner about a block away."

"What is your name? My name is Tina."

"That's a pretty name. My name is kind of old-fashioned. It's Sarah."

" I like old-fashioned names. They make me think of some of the movies like westerns that we see on TV sometimes."

"Do you go to school around here?" Sarah asked.

"No, I lived in upstate New York. My father was killed in a train accident and I had to go live with my grandma because my mom had to work. She just lost her job and we're going out to Arizona to see if she can get a job out there. Some friends of hers are sending us the plane tickets and we can stay with them until we get a place of our own."

"Gee, that sounds exciting! I wish something like that would happen to me."

"Do you know Jesus? We feel like he worked all this out for us because we didn't know what we were going to do."

"Who is Jesus? I never heard of him."

"Jesus is the Son of God. He came to earth and died on a cross so that we could be saved and he could take care of us."

"How does a person get to know him?"

"Do you know how to pray?"

"No, what is that?"

"Prayer is talking to Jesus."

"Could you show me how?"

"Yes, let's just hold hands like this." She reached over and grasped Sarah's hand. "Now bow your head and repeat after me. 'Dear Jesus. I want to know you and take you as my Savior. Please forgive me for all my sins and help me not to do them anymore. In your precious name, I ask it and I know you heard my prayer." As Tina continued to hold Sarah's hand she repeated everything Tina had told her. As she finished her prayer both girls were crying with tears running down their faces. Tammy stood in the doorway listening, tears running down her cheeks also. Tina put her arms around Sarah and hugged her.

Sarah said, "I feel so clean just like somebody had washed my soul!"

"He really has! And all you have to do if you have a problem is go to him like you just did and He will answer you. "

"That's right!" Tammy said, as she came into the room.

She placed glasses and a plate of cookies on the table and turned to hug Sarah. "You must give us your name and address and phone number so we can keep in touch with you."

"Yes" Tina joined in. "Maybe we can have you come out and visit us."

"Do you go to church anywhere?' Tammy asked her.

"No. I haven't ever."

"Would you like us to find a church or meeting where you could go to get prayer when you need help?'

"Oh, yes! Can you do that?"

"Just give us your full name and address and phone number, if you have one and we'll see that someone gets in touch with you this week! Just a minute. I'll get some paper and a pen. Make two copies. One for us to take with us so we can keep in touch with you and one for the person who will see that you get involved in a group of Christian young people." She handed the notepaper to Sarah and waited until she had written everything down. As Sarah handed her the papers, Tammy said, "Now, let's sit down and have some cookies and a glass of lemonade."

"I see by your address that you are living with someone other than your parents. Are you a foster child?"

"Yes".

"Do you know where your parents are?"

"Not really. I think they're dead. I can't remember them."

"Have you always lived with these same people?"

"No. I just live in foster homes. I've never lived in the same home more than six months at a time. I never met people like you and Tina before."

"Hmmn! Well, I think something is cooking in my head and I have an idea what God wants us to do when we get to Phoenix. If I'm right, we'll have a great big house where we can bring girls like you and give them a real home. I'm not promising anything but this is something we should all pray about. I'll tell the group I've been worshipping with and they'll pray about it, too. Both of you girls pray earnestly that God will lead us in what He wants done."

"Oh, Tammy! You give me hope! I just feel that God is going to do something wonderful. Now that I've learned how to pray, I'm going to do a lot of it!"

"There's one more thing. You need a Bible to read and I think it should be a Living Bible. A father made this translation for his son and had it published so that young people could understand the Bible better. I'll ask him to get one and bring it to you tomorrow. I have a friend that's coming to help us tomorrow and I'll ask him to go buy you one so you be sure and come over after school tomorrow and we'll have it for you.

"I'll be here. I sure wish I'd met you a long time ago."

"Everything comes about in God's time. Sometimes He lets things happen in our lives so we'll have sympathy for others when it happens to them and just like Tina did with you today, they know what to do when the need arises. Watch and pray and God will use you in the same way.."

"Oh, I will! I know a lot of girls that are going down the same path that I was. They need Jesus to turn them around.. I'd better get home now or I'll be in the doghouse there. I don't believe they know about Jesus either. Pray that I'll be able to witness to them. I love you both." She cried as she hugged them and then ran out of the apartment.

Tammy gathered Tina in her arms and they both wept and prayed together. "You know, Tina. I never knew you could talk to someone like that. I'm so proud of you. Here I was worried about her influence on you, and you knew what to do all the time."

"I guess I got a pretty good upbringing with grandma. She really knew how to pray and she taught me how."

"We'll have to write and tell her about Sarah. She sure will be proud.. Now we'd better get us some supper and make a couple of phone calls. One to Robert and one to Howard and Ella."

CHAPTER TWENTY-ONE

Their dinner over and the kitchen cleaned up, Tammy picked up the phone and called Howard. "Howard, this is Tammy," she said when he answered.

"I'm glad you called now. Did you get the tickets?"

"No, we didn't so I thought I'd better call you and see what we are supposed to do."

"Well, the airlines called me and said not to worry. They will have the tickets right there at the reservation desk, all you have to do is pick them up and get registered. You should be at the airport an hour before your departure which is at seven A.M. I know that's awfully early but that is the plane's schedule."

"That's all right. Robert is coming to take us to the airport and I know he will be willing to come whenever it's necessary. Did I tell you he sold my car for one thousand dollars? That will be a big help until I can get a job."

"That is great! But we don't want you to worry about a thing. Just relax and take your time getting settled. I'm certain the Lord already has everything worked out. Just trust Him!"

"Talk about everything being worked out. Tina led a girl to the Lord yesterday and I think the Lord wants me to start a home for girls like her. She can't remember her parents and has been living in foster homes all her life. She doesn't know anything else. She says she's never lived in any foster home for more than six months at a time."

"That is remarkable! Ella and I have been taking classes at church for just such a project. Who knows what will come of it? You know the Pastor's son has done that in California. Maybe he will help us to get one started in the Phoenix area. I'd like to see a ranch for both boys and girls started."

"Oh, Howard, what an idea! Well, I'd better not hold the phone up any longer and I need to call Robert and tell him about the time. Give Ella and Dorothy my love and tell them we'll see them tomorrow. 'Bye,"

"Goodbye. I'll meet you at the airport. God bless you!"

CHAPTER TWENTY-TWO

Tammy turned to speak to Tina but found her asleep on the sofa. She shook her awake and told her to go up to bed as they would have to get up at five A.M. Then she picked up the phone to call Robert.

"Hello? This is Robert."

"This is Tammy, Robert. I just talked to Howard and he says the airline will have the tickets at the reservation desk. All we have to do is pick them up and get registered. Our plane leaves at seven A.M. and we have to be there an hour early so we need to leave here around five. Will that be OK with you?"

"That will be fine with me. I'll be there a few minutes before five. Everything will be OK."

"There's another thing I need to talk to you about also.

Tina led a young girl to the Lord yesterday. I think she's about thirteen years old and has lived in foster homes all her life. She can't remember her parents; doesn't even know who they were. She had never heard of Jesus until Tina talked to her. Will you see that our group sort of takes her under their wing until I can have her brought out to Phoenix? I just talked with Howard and he's thinking about starting a ranch for boys and girls like her. The Lord was leading me along the same lines."

"I would love to be involved in something like that!".

Robert replied. "We sure will watch over her until you're able to find a place for her out there. I might even come out there later on and help in such an enterprise. I think this is what God has been preparing me for. You have her name and address and everything?"

"Yes, I had her make two copies so I could give one to you and one for ourselves so we can keep in touch with her."

"Okay. I'll see you in the morning. Have a good night's sleep."

"Good night and God bless you real good!"

Tammy hung up, turned off the lights and made her way to her bedroom. She undressed, turned off the light and climbed into bed. Covering herself up against the chill of the night, she closed her eyes and began to pray. "Dear Jesus, how we thank you for the changes you are making in our lives. Thank you for Sarah. We're sure you sent her our way on purpose. Please keep her safe until we can send for her and, if it's your will for us to be involved in making a ranch for boys and girls like her, give us the wisdom to do whatever you tell us to do and we will be forever grateful to you. Help me to remember to tithe on the thousand dollars you gave me for the car. Help us both to sleep soundly so that we'll be rested for our journey. Bless Robert for all the help he's given us. Help him to know and be obedient to you will. Thank you again so much. I love you. Amen"

She had almost fallen asleep as she prayed and was deep in slumber as she turned over and snuggled down in the blankets.

CHAPTER TWENTY-THREE

Having set the alarm for four-thirty A.M. Tammy was roused from sleep as it rang. She hurried to waken Tina.
"Tina, wake up. Time to get ready. Robert will be here at five and we have to be ready to leave."

Tina groaned and tried to burrow deeper under the covers but Tammy knew they just didn't have time for that. She pulled the covers off and said, "Tina, you must get up now! C'mon."

Tina roused and went to the bathroom to wash the sleep out of her eyes. "Sorry, Mom," she said. "I just couldn't seem to wake up. I'll be ready in time. Do you suppose we could pick up some doughnuts or something at the airport?"

"Yes, they have little shops there. We'll get something. I should have got something last night but we had so many things to do. Right now we must have our luggage ready for Robert to put in the car and I have to lock up and take the keys over to the lady in the other apartment. I'm afraid she won't be too happy to be waked up this early in the morning." Both of them continued to dress as they talked and were soon ready to leave when Robert got there. Since it was quite cold in New York they got their warm coats on and sat waiting for him. It wasn't too long before they heard his car door slam and they knew it was time for them to be on their way. They put their luggage in the hall and Tammy went next door to leave the keys with her neighbor. The neighbor was up waiting for her and Tammy thanked her for losing sleep for them.

"That's all right", the neighbor replied. "I was glad to do it. Have a good trip."

"Thank you." I'm sure we will. God bless you."

Just then Robert came up and grabbed their luggage. Tina and Tammy followed him to the car. Tammy opened her purse after they were settled in the car and had fastened their seat belts. " Thank you for coming for us. I don't know what we would have done without you. Here" she said as she handed him the slip of paper with Sarah's address on it. "Will you be sure to get her a Living Bible?"

And could you call me at Howard's if there is any problem? I have a feeling that the foster parents aren't too good to her. They might resent what they would call meddling by a church group."

"Good morning to you, too! I didn't say anything because you were talking to your neighbor and I didn't want to prolong the conversation. Sorry about that!"

"And good morning to you," Tammy replied. "I've been trying to remember if I wrote down Howard's address and phone number for you. Did I?"

"Yes. In fact, Howard gave it to me. I'll keep you posted about Sarah. As long as she is OK, I won't call but I'm thinking I might be able to talk to the foster parents and perhaps win them to the Lord."

"Oh, that would be wonderful! We'll be praying about that, too."

"We'll be at the airport in just a few more minutes." Robert said. " I'll let you out in front of the airline and then go park the car. A porter will take your luggage to the registration desk. I should be back in here by then and can help you with your tickets if you need me."

"OK" replied Tammy. "We'll wait for you there but I don't think you'll be allowed through the gate. Security is so tight now. The last I flew, I even had to take my shoes off. You couldn't take a fingernail file or anything like that."

"Yes, I know. Ever since 9/11 they've been having tighter and tighter restrictions. Since I won't be able to go through the gate with you, I suggest we have prayer before

I leave and I want to assure you that I will be praying for you all the way. Will you call me when you get to Howard's house. It will be a load off my mind to know you're safe."

Tammy and the Pharmacist

"Yes, I'm sure Howard will insist that I call and let you know when we get to his house. "I'll need to call Mom, too, and let her know we're all right."

"Well, here we are. Let me get your luggage out and then I'll park and be right back."

A porter came over to load their luggage on a cart as Robert drove the car to the parking lot. "Which airline, ma'am?" he asked.

I think it's American Airlines going to Phoenix, Arizona leaving at 7 AM. My tickets are to be at the reservation desk."

"Fine. If you'll just follow me, I'll take you right there."

Tammy and Tina followed him to the reservation desk where he loaded their luggage to be weighed. By that time Robert was back and ready to help if he was needed and to pray before saying goodbye.

Their tickets were there as Howard had said they would be. Tammy signed in and the agent weighed her luggage and, then gave her identification tags so she could retrieve them at her destination. Putting the tickets in her purse, she kept the 'boarding passes in her hand and turned to Robert.

He led them to one side and all three bowed their heads as Robert prayed that God would be with them on this trip and keep them safe as they traveled. Then giving them each a hug, he turned to leave. "I find it hard to let you go but I'm confident that we will be seeing each other real soon. I'll get the Bible for Sarah and talk to her foster parents. I think, too, it would be wise to talk to the authorities and see if there is any reason she couldn't make the trip out to Phoenix in the near future. I kinda think I may escort her myself when you give the word."

"Oh, Robert! That would be just perfect. Keep me posted. I don't know whether Howard has a computer or not. If not, maybe I can take some of that money from the car and buy an inexpensive one. E-mail would be so much easier to communicate by."

"I agree with that. Well, it's time to say goodbye. God bless and keep you and if He wills it I'll see you real soon."

Tammy and Tina headed for the gate where they would depart and Robert left the building to go to his car.

Tammy and the Pharmacist

As they reached the gate, they had to pass through and have all their carry on luggage and purse scanned. Fortunately there were no problems. They still had almost a half hour left to boarding time so Tammy looked for a place to buy something for breakfast. They found a small shop that sold doughnuts and coffee or hot chocolate. Tammy purchased a bag of doughnuts, a cup of hot coffee for herself and a cup of hot chocolate for Tina. They carried it back to the gate and sat down to eat while they waited for their plane.

Since it was such an early flight, many others were doing the same thing. They had barely finished when the attendant at the gate announced that their flight would be boarding. They followed the rest of the people through the Jetway to the door of the plane. Several people were in wheel chairs and they were taken on first. As they found their seats, Tina wanted to sit next to the window so Tammy took the seat next to her. This was Tina's first plane trip and she was very excited. All the people were finally aboard and had found their seats. The seat belt sign came on alerting everyone to fasten them and sit upright in their seats. Then the captain began to rev up the engine. Backing out of it's stall, the plane lined up for take-off behind several other planes that were waiting. Soon the other planes were in the air and their plane was revving it's engines waiting for the signal from the tower.

Although those in the cabin of the plane couldn't hear the conversation from the tower, in just a few minutes their plane was shooting down the runway and climbed into the air. It kept climbing until it was above the clouds, then leveled off and passengers were able to undo their seat belts and put their seats back if they so desired. Soon the attendants pushed carts into the aisle and began to distribute snacks and soft drinks. Nothing like the old days when you could get a full course dinner, especially if you were riding first class! Tina would never experience that but Tammy remembered the old days when flying was a big experience. Someone turned on the TV and Tina turned to listen. Soon she tired of it and put her seat back.

Tammy asked the stewardess for a pillow for her and it wasn't long before Tina was snoozing. Tammy, however, although she was tired, didn't feel like she could sleep. There were too many things on her mind. She closed her eyes and began to pray silently that God would have his way in her life and his will would be done in everything she did. Finally, she did doze off for a while. When she woke up it was after eleven AM. She checked her watch and realized they only had about two more hours until they reached Phoenix.

Tina was watching television. "How long will it be before we reach Phoenix, Mom?" she asked.

"About two hours." Tammy replied.

"This is really great!" exclaimed Tina. "Look how beautiful the clouds are! And you see glimpses of the ground sometimes. Automobiles look like ants crawling along the highways. What an experience this is."

"Yes, and you'll be surprised by the change in climate. It's much warmer and Phoenix is surrounded by mountains in which there are beautiful lakes. You can go swimming or fishing, if you like. I think you're going to like it there."

"Oh, I do, too! I can hardly wait. I hope your plans to make a ranch where girls and boys like Sarah can come happens quickly. I'm anxious to meet Dorothy and her mother and Howard. I've never even met him."

"Well, it won't be long now. Our plane should be landing in another hour. Howard will be there to meet us. I don't think Ella or Dorothy will be with him as Dorothy will be in school. And, if I know Ella, she'll be fixing lunch for us."

CHAPTER TWENTY-FOUR

Soon the stewardess was telling everyone to fasten their seat belts and put their head rest in an upright position as the plane would be landing in about twenty minutes. It seemed a very short time when the plane began to lose altitude and you could see buildings and roads. Tina watched out the window in excitement. "Look, Mom, there's the airport and a long, long runway. "Ooh, we're landing."

"Yes, it will be just a few more minutes now. You can't unfasten your seat belt yet. We have to wait until the plane taxis up to the Jetway and quits moving. "

"OK, Mom. It's quit moving now. Can we get our belongings and get out in the aisle now?

"Yes, Just don't push ahead of people. They're all anxious to get out. I think Howard will meet us where we pick up our luggage. That will take quite a while, too."

"Oh, this so exciting."

"Stay close to me. We don't want to get separated."

"OK, Mom!"

"Well, we're finally out of the plane and we just need to watch for the signs pointing to where we pick up our luggage. I'm sure Howard will be there to meet us."

"There's the sign, Mom! Is that Howard coming toward us?"

"Yes, that's him! Wave to him. Ah, he sees us!"

"Tammy and Tina! I thought that was you." He said as he hugged both of them. "Your luggage should be coming soon. Ella stayed home so she could fix lunch. Also, she figured you'd need the space in the car. We'll be on our way as soon as we get your luggage. Did you have a good trip?"

"Oh, it was wonderful!" Tina piped up.

"Is that your luggage coming through right now? "

"I believe it is." Tammy replied. "Yes, that's it."

Howard snatched the luggage as it passed by. Is this all of it?"

"No, I think there's one more bag." Tammy said. "Yes, there it is."

Howard grabbed it up and they went out to the parking lot to get his car. When they were all in he drove to the gate and paid his fee, then drove out toward the highway.

"Gee, we're way up high," Tina cried.

"Yes, the airport is in the mountains. That's why they call it Sky Harbor."

"Wow. Everything is sure different here."

Tammy laughed. "You'll find a lot of things that are different here."

"That's for sure." Howard said. "Well, we're on our way. It will only take us about half an hour since we're over the line in Glendale. Fasten your seatbelts. Here we come."

"Y'know, last week this time, I never dreamed I'd be out here and that Tina would be with me. What a difference when you're trusting the Lord. He can make things happen so soon, it takes your breath away!"

"I've found that out!" Howard replied. "I understand Robert might be coming out here to live and wants to become involved in a project to help youngsters like Tina and the girl (Sarah, I believe,) to find a new life in Jesus.?"

"Yes, that's what he said this morning when he brought us to the airport. He has a call from God on his life just like you have." Tammy replied. "He believes God wants him to come here, too."

"Do you know how soon?" Howard asked.

"No, I don't think even he knows that yet. He just knows it's the kind of thing he feels God is leading him to do. For now, he will concentrate on trying to reach Sarah's foster parents. Then he'd like to come out here and help us get a ranch started for boys and girls like Sarah."

Tammy and the Pharmacist

"Wow! When God moves and motivates people, He sure does it in a big way. No pussy-footing around. Don't just say it. *Do it!*" Howard replied. "Well, here we are," he said as he pulled into the driveway of his home.

Ella came running out as Howard pulled up and his passengers climbed out of the car.. "Tammy! I'm so glad you got here OK. (She put her arms around her and hugged her,) And this is Tina?" she asked as she hugged her, too.

"Come on in the house while Howard brings your luggage in. I have lunch all ready. I imagine you're pretty hungry."

"Yeah, we are kind of hungry," Tammy said.

"Kinda? I'm starved." Tina cried.

Ella laughed. "You sound just like Dorothy. She'll be home for lunch in a few minutes so you can get to know each other."

"Well, the luggage is all in the house. Let's go in and let these gals get situated."

"Okay. C'mon." Ella added.

They had just entered the house when Dorothy came bursting through the door. "Oh, I'm so happy you're here! she cried. "I know you're Tammy so this must be Tina! Right?'

Laughing, Tina answered, "Right!" Then they hugged. "Now I've got a sister." Dorothy declared.

Everybody laughed and Ella urged them to sit down to the table. She brought out macaroni salad, tuna sandwiches, lemonade and big slices of banana bread.

Tina groaned, "Now I know I'm in heaven."

Howard said, "Shall we bow our heads for the blessing?

"Our precious Savior, we offer our sacrifice of praise to thee. We thank thee for the safe arrival of our guests and for the way you have blessed them. We also thank you for this food which Ella has prepared with loving hands. May we enjoy our sojourn together as we endeavor to serve thee in a greater way. Amen."

The girls kept up an animated conversation as they partook of this sumptuous luncheon. The adults hardly had a chance to get a word in edgewise. Finally, Ella said to Tammy, "Howard tells me that the young man who led him to the Lord is planning on coming

Tammy and the Pharmacist

out here also. That he wants to start a ranch for boys and girls like the one you just led to the Lord. What's her name? Sarah, I believe?"

"Yes, Robert is looking out for her now and is going to try to win her foster parents to the Lord. And, of course, as soon as he can get settled out here, he plans on sending for her to come, too. It will all depend on what kind of help we can get here for such a project but I think your minister is adept at such things and we're hoping to enlist his aid."

"By the way" Howard broke in. "Tonight is prayer meeting. Would you be interested in going after you get rested up a bit?"

"Oh, yes, I would. Tina napped on the plane but I think I might take a little nap so I'll be fresh this evening."

"Then, if you are all finished eating, why don't we show you where you will sleep so you can get your luggage put away and so forth.' Ella said. " Dorothy has to go back to school but she will be back home at 2:30. Do you plan on entering Tina in school tomorrow? I'm sure she will enjoy it there. It's just around the block so they're able to come home for lunch."

"Wow, I'd forgotten about entering her in school but I suppose it's a good idea to get her started right away. Yes, I'd like to do it tomorrow before I start looking for a job. I'll need to look for an inexpensive car, too., so I can get around."

"Don't worry about that right now. Howard has his own car and you can use mine. I don't go that much. In fact, I could take him to work and keep his car, if we happen to need them both, isn't that right, Howard?"

"Certainly."

"Okay, let's go upstairs then and I'll show you where you are to sleep. Tina will share Dorothy's room as she has twin beds. This is her room. Tina, you will find some empty drawers. You can put your things away. There are also empty hangers in the closet."

"Thank you," Tina replied. "This is a lovely room. I'm sure we'll have a lot of fun together."

"Tammy, this is your room." She opened the door to a spacious room with a double bed, dresser and night –stand all in white with touches of gold on the drawer pulls and above the mirror. The walls were a light blue and the printed draperies had a white background with sprays of pink and lilac flowers among the pale green leaves that trailed among them. "Like Tina's room there are empty drawers and plenty of hangers in the closet. I hope you will be happy here."

"What a lovely, serene setting! I love it already. You may have a hard time getting rid of me when I'm able to get a place of my own. Thank you so much." Tammy cried as she hugged Ella.

"There is a bathroom between the two bedrooms for you and the girls to share. Howard and I have our own in the master suite. Now why don't Howard and I go downstairs and let you take a nap?"

"I'm so excited I don't know whether I'll be able to sleep or not. You are being so wonderful. I'll never be able to repay you!"

"Just let the Lord take care of that. He's the one who is behind all this. I'll call you about five, if you're not awake before then."

"OK, I appreciate that! Thank you again."

Howard and Ella went down stairs so their guests could rest.

Ella tidied up the kitchen, putting the soiled dishes in the dishwasher. She went in the living room and turned the TV on low. There was a Christian program that she wanted to see. She had dinner all planned and it wouldn't take her long to get it ready later. Howard decided to run down to the pharmacy to see what the situation was there but Tom had everything under control. Seeing he was not really needed he decided to go back home and rest up for the evening.

CHAPTER TWENTY-FIVE

Ella was just starting to prepare dinner. Dorothy had come home from school and was watching television as she waited for Tina to wake up. Soon Tammy awoke and roused Tina. They both used the bathroom to freshen up and then came downstairs. Dorothy and Tina began to talk excitedly about Tina's debut at the school next day. Dorothy was so excited about taking her new friend to meet the teachers and principal. She'd already told a lot of her friends about Tina and was anxious to introduce her to them. Of course, Tina was looking forward to that, too.

Tammy went into the kitchen to see if she could help Ella. "Yes. You and the girls can set the table if you'd like. Dinner is almost ready and I understand you and Howard both are anxious to talk to the pastor about the ideas you have for a ranch for homeless boys and girls. It sounds like a wonderful idea to me. I'll get dinner on the table right away so we can go early."

As soon as dinner was over, they tidied up the kitchen, then piled in to the car and took off for church. The pastor had just arrived when they got there and Howard introduced his guests to him. Tammy was thrilled to meet this great man who had done so much to further the kingdom of the Lord. She could hardly wait to talk to him about their dream of building a ranch for homeless boys and girls, not just in Phoenix but anywhere in the United States where the need was greatest, especially in New York. She was hoping to get a job right away so she could get a car and a home for Tina and herself. When Robert came out they could begin to look into purchasing ground. She hoped they'd be able to find land with a small lake on it. She remembered the only river in that area was the Colorado River and much of that was in the Grand Canyon.

How wonderful it would be if they could find such a place. Maybe the Lord had one already picked out! She was so engrossed in her dream that she didn't hear the pastor address her.

"Oh, I'm sorry," she said. "I didn't mean to be rude. I'm just so excited about the burden the Lord has laid on our hearts to build a ranch for boys and girls here. Do you already have plans along that line?"

"Not exactly a ranch but we are concerned about having a place where homeless children can come. I think your perspective is greater than any of us had dreamed of as yet. However, there are those who would pitch in and help if God put these plans into being.! I'd suggest that we have a special meeting with all those who are concerned about this and see what they come up with. Do you have any idea when Robert intends to come out? "

"No," Tammy answered but I think he wants to come as soon as he can possibly wind things up back in New York and he's interested in bringing Sarah out,too, as soon as we have a place for her to come to. He'll have to talk to the authorities there since she's a foster child. I'm sure they'll look into his background and check his credentials. I have to get Tina installed in school tomorrow, then I'm hoping to get a job at Motorola. "

"You sure have everything cut out for you. We'll be praying that you'll be successful. What does Robert do for a living?"

'He is a super car salesman and I don't think he'll have any problem finding employment."

"Where do you fit in all this Howard?"

"Well, I'm thrilled with the possibilities and I know if God wants something done, he'll find the persons to do it and he'll also supply the means! Our part is to find those persons and correlate everything together for the purpose that God intended. I think he sent Tammy out here on purpose and laid this burden on her heart!"

"I say, 'Amen ' to that! Well, how about bringing this matter up at our meeting next Thursday evening and we'll see what the consensus of opinion is and what resources we have that can be channeled in to it. There's a possibility that someone in a congregation this large might have a piece of property with exactly what we need that they will be willing to donate! You just never know what God will do!"

"Yes, and it's so exciting to watch and see how everything comes together. All we have to do is have faith." Howard replied. " There's a song we sing that says 'prayer is the key to heaven but *FAITH unlocks the door!* ' We can pray until we're blue in the face but if we don't believe it, no results will occur,"

"That is so right! Well, it's time to start the Prayer meeting. We have a lot to pray about tonight, as usual."

After the song service, Pastor called Tammy and Tina up and introduced them to the congregation. Later, people crowded around to greet them and welcome them to their midst,

That night, when they got home, Howard asked Tammy if she'd like to call Robert and find out how he came out concerning Sarah and to report the progress they had made so far.

"Oh, yes, I would like to call him. I've been real worried about Sarah. Not that I think she'd get into trouble but that the foster parents might resent any interference on the part of a Christian organization. Let me get his phone number out of my purse."

She came back with the number and took the phone to call. "Robert? This is Tammy. How are you doing?"

"Meaning – 'what's up with Sarah? Well, you'll be glad to know that she's still with the foster parents and they don't seem to have any animosity toward me. I think it will take a little while to break down any resistance to the gospel, though. We'll just have to leave that with the Lord. So! How did your trip go and are you all situated?"

"Yes, we're all settled for the time being here with Howard and Ella and their daughter. Tina is delirious with joy. She'll be going to school tomorrow. The biggest news I have to tell you is that the Pastor is having a meeting next Thursday night to discuss our plans for building a ranch for home-less boys and girls. He's hoping there might be someone willing to donate land! He wants to know when you plan to come out. Could you possibly manage to fly out for a few days, maybe a weekend?"

"Whoa! You're going too fast for me. I'll have to see if I can get plane reservations but I'd sure like to be in on that meeting! I'll get on the internet after I hang up and see if I can get tickets. Then I'll call you back and let you know. You and Howard and the rest had better pray that I'll sell a few more cars!"

"OK, We'll wait for your call. 'Bye for now."

Turning to Howard and Ella, she said "Wow! Maybe he'll fly out for that meeting next week. He's getting on the internet now to see whether he can get plane reservations. Meanwhile, is it OK if I call my Mom and let her know we got here safe?"

"Sure," Howard replied. "Go right ahead."

"Thank you." Tammy dialed her mother's phone.

"Hello?"

"Hi, Mom. I just wanted to let you know we got here OK and are all settled in. Tina is in seventh heaven. She just loves it here and will be entered in school with Dorothy tomorrow. I plan on going out to Motorola tomorrow after I get her settled and see if I can get a job there. Then, when we got home Sunday night Robert Warren was there. He's the one who led Howard to the Lord. Anyway he'd like to come out here too and we're talking about building a ranch for homeless boys and girls. Howard and I talked with the Pastor of this big church we'll be attending and he's going to present this plan for a ranch to a meeting of some of the members next Thursday night. He thinks someone might donate the land. The church has about two thousand members and he also thinks there might be those who would help finance it. Isn't that wonderful?"

"You make me wish I'd come, too!"

"Well, you can always come later when we have a house to bring you to. For now, we're full up."

"I just might sell my house and help you get a house out there. How would you like that?"

"You know I'd love that, Mom. Just take it to the Lord in prayer. He'll show you what to do. He'll help you sell it, too!"

"All right, honey. I'll do that. Now, I'd better let you go.: We don't want to run Howard's phone bills up."

"Bye, Mom, I love you."

She had just hung up when the phone rang again. Howard indicated she should answer it. It was Robert calling back.

"Tammy, I got tickets for Wednesday next week. Same time your flight was. I'll plan on staying for the weekend and fly back here on

Sunday afternoon. There's a flight at 3:30 P.M. That way, I'll be able to stay for the morning service. Will you ask Howard to find me a motel and make reservations for those four nights? I can rent a car while I'm there so he won't need to worry about transportation.'

"Okay, we'll do that. I look forward to your visit. Who knows what God will do? 'It's the most exciting life I've ever lived!"

"Me, too. Bye for now!"

"Bye." She put the phone down and turned to Howard and Ella. "Robert will be coming Wednesday on the same plane we flew out on. He wants to know if you'll make reservations for him at a motel near here. He says he'll rent a car when he gets here and he will fly back to New York on Sunday afternoon. And Mom is talking about selling her house and helping me buy one here. Praise the Lord!"

"You know," Howard said, "When the Lord starts something, he doesn't waste any time! Things move! Hallelujah"

CHAPTER TWENTY-SIX

Thursday morning they were all up early, had breakfast and were ready to go in their various directions. Ella offered to take Tammy and Tina over to school along with Dorothy. Then drive her to Motorola to put in her application for a job. Tammy accepted graciously as she didn't want to offend her benefactress. Howard had offered prayer as they ate their breakfast and had already gone to his business. School started at 8:30 AM there so they left right away.

At the school, Ella showed Tammy and Tina where the office was and introduced them to the secretary then settled down in the outer office to wait for them.

"Do you have your papers from the other school?" the secretary queried.

"No, but I have the address of the school and everything you will need to send for them." Tammy replied. "We had to make this transition so suddenly that there was no time to get papers as I went to bring her home on the weekend."

"Oh? And where was home to you and where was Tina located?"

"I lived and worked in New York City. Tina lived with my mother in Scarsdale, New York. I had to go get her so I could bring her out here with me. I worked at Macy's in the Auditing Department. When that department was dissolved and turned over to an Auditing Agency, my job was dissolved. Mr. and Mrs. Peters insisted that we come out and stay with them until I could get a job and a place to live. I went to high school here. You could probably get my records, if necessary. We knew both the Peters back then."

"And your husband?"

"My husband was killed last year in a train accident in New York. Maybe you read about it."

"Oh, yes, I did. I don't mean to be suspicious but we have to very careful when we are entering students in the school."

"Yes, I realize that and I'm grateful for it. It's good to know that you're keeping a strict account of our children."

"All right, let's get your daughter's name, date of birth, and the name of her school."

"Name?"

"Tina Sue Waring."

"Date of birth?"

"May 15" 1994.

"Name of school?"

"Scarsdale Middle School."

"Okay," the secretary said. "I think that will be enough information to send to the Board of Education there. I'll get the papers off today by computer. If you can come back Friday morning, I'm sure she can be entered then. I can't put her in a class yet until I know what grade level, etc. she will belong in. Can she go with you now?

"Yes, of course." She rose to go. "We'll see you tomorrow morning."

Ella rose as Tammy and Tina came out of the office, a question on her face. "They couldn't put her in a class until they get her records from her old school. They'll get them by computer today and we'll have to come back in the morning."

"Well, she'll just have to come with us then," Ella replied. "Let's go."

The three of them hurried out to the car and sped away to Motorola so Tammy could put her application in there.

At Motorola, Ella and Tina waited in the waiting room while Tammy went in to inquire. They waited quite a while and Tammy didn't come out.

"Maybe they're doing an interview right now." Ella remarked. "That would be wonderful."

Tammy and the Pharmacist

"Yes, we never know how God will work things out. I never dreamed we'd have trouble getting in to the school. I thought you just walked in and said you wanted to go to school there and they assigned you to a class! Live and learn, right?"

"That's right," Ella responded. "I guess God thought this was more important right now. I'm sure they'll have everything tomorrow morning for you."

"Oh, here she comes now and she's smiling. Looks like she might have good news."

They rose to their feet as she came up to them. "I think I may have a job in the office. They just want to check with my records at Macy's. I gave them your address and phone number. They'll call me as soon as they get the records but it sounds real favorable."

They went out to the car. As they climbed in and settled themselves, Ella asked, "Is there anywhere else where you'd like to go now?"

"Not really." Tammy replied. "Does Howard usually come home for lunch? I know Dorothy does."

"Yes, they both do. OK, I guess we'd better head for home then. "Any time you want to shop or anything you can take the car. Just let me know in time so I can make other plans if I'm going anywhere."

"OK, "Tammy replied. "You know, I haven't set my watch back to Arizona time. What time do you have now?

"I have eleven fifteen." Ella replied.

"Thanks, I'll set my watch back right now so I don't get confused. There! Now I'm on Arizona time. Do you have yours set, Tina? '

"Yes, Mom. I set it last night."

"You always are one step ahead of me." Tammy laughed.

"Looks like we'll be right on time to fix lunch before Dorothy and Howard get here. " Ella commented as she turned into the driveway.

It was not long before both Howard and Dorothy appeared and as they all sat down at the table, Howard returned 'Thanks ' to the Lord, then turned to Tammy to find out what progress they'd had this morning.

"Well," Tammy replied. "It was just about what you'd normally expect. Since we left without notice, we didn't have any papers for Tina. They are sending for them by computer. We'll have to go back tomorrow to get her entered. Motorola was very favorable and I think I will have a job there. They said I could expect to hear in a day or so, probably not until Monday."

"Well, I consider that pretty good news," Howard replied. "Do you want to go to that meeting at the church tonight?"

"Yes. I think we'll need every contact we can get. Besides I want to get in the habit of attending certain meetings."

"That's right. We have been doing that and we find it very beneficial in our Christian walk. Both Ella and Dorothy are involved in different types of ministries. I'm sure Tina will enjoy those ministries also."

"I'm sure I will, too," Tina piped up. "I can't wait to get really involved."

"That's great, "Howard replied, "now I guess Dorothy and I had better get back to our respective positions. Ready, Dorothy?"

:"Yes, Daddy. Are you going to drop me off?"

"Sure. Let's go. 'Bye for now."

As they left, Ella and Tammy gathered up the leavings of lunch and disposed of them.

"Is there anything you'd like to do this afternoon?" Ella asked Tammy.

"Not really," Tammy replied. "I think I'll finish reading the book I brought on the plane and maybe take a short nap. Is there anything I can do for you?"

"No. I'll probably do the same thing after I put a roast in the crock pot with some vegetables. They can be cooking while we rest."

Just then the phone rang. Ella answered it and found it was for Tammy. She handed the phone, "It's for you," she said.

"Hello?" Tammy said, as she lifted the receiver to her ear. "Oh, thank you. I didn't expect to hear so soon. When do you want me to come in?"

"How about ten o'clock tomorrow? Will that be convenient? "

" Yes, it will. I have to take my daughter to school at eight o'clock to get her signed in. We did the preliminary work today so it shouldn't take too long. I believe I can make it to Motorola by ten."

"If you prefer, we can make it for ten-thirty."

"Perhaps that would be better. I sure don't want to be late for my first appointment."

"Good. We'll see you then."

Tammy hung up the phone and turned to Ella. "Isn't our Lord wonderful? That was Motorola calling me to come in for an interview tomorrow! I can hardly believe it.

So soon!"

"Oh, that's wonderful! You can take the car tomorrow. That way, you'll be able to go wherever you need to at whatever time." Ella offered.

"Thank you. Well, I guess I'll go up and talk to the Lord a little bit, then read until I'm sleepy and take a nap."

"Sounds like a good plan. I'll call you in time for dinner."

CHAPTER TWENTY-SEVEN

After dinner that evening they hurried to get ready to go to the special meeting at church. Tina and Dorothy would attend the one especially for youth while Howard, Ella and Tammy went to the other meeting in the sanctuary.

Pastor Bob, the Senior pastor was chairing the meeting tonight. He asked Howard if he would lead them in prayer. Howard stood to his feet. "Father, as we come together this evening, we lift our hearts to thee in praise and thanksgiving for all that you do for us; how you supply all our needs in abundance. Tonight as we pray for your direction and for those who are in need of healing or financial needs or direction for their lives, give us thy grace, help each person concerned to really believe, to really have FAITH, for it's faith that unlocks the door to Heaven. Thank you for hearing us pray."

There was a chorus of amens. Then Pastor Bob asked for Prayer requests. There were many for healing, not only for themselves but, also, for friends and neighbors. Many requests were for jobs and financial help. Tammy put in a request for boys and girls that were on the streets, many who were missing. She reminded them of the cards that came in the mail picturing a lost child, that they should pray over each picture of a child shown there.

As the group remained on their knees before the Lord many prayers rose, like a sweet incense to heaven, for friends, loved ones, acquaintances, and especially for those who didn't know Jesus as their Savior. Finally, they became silent as they listened to the Lord.

Then Pastor Bob said Amen and they got up from their knees and sat down in their seats. "Next week we will be addressing a special problem that faces every community, that of children who are left to roam the streets with no homes, no food, no one to love or care for them. We have a responsibility to them, for our Lord said, "Bring the little children unto me, and forbid them not, for of such is the kingdom of heaven". Pray about this all week, ask God what your part should be and what we, as a congregation should do, what is *our responsibility.* Then, when we come back next week, we will discuss what God has told us to do. A young man, Robert Warren, from New York will be here to discuss it with us as well as our own Howard Peters, whom you already know. Now, God bless you as you go to your homes. Goodnight."

Howard, Tammy and Ella went to pick up the girls and then back toward home. "I know girls like you usually like to have a treat when they're out. Would you like to stop at a Dairy Queen and get a milkshake or dish of ice cream?"

"Yeah," they both cried.

"What about us?" Ella asked.

Howard laughed. "Of course, we'll have some, too."

He pulled in to the Dairy Queen and asked for their order."

"May I have a chocolate milk shake." Tina asked

"Me, too." Dorothy ordered.

"I'd like a strawberry milk shake," Ella said.

"Ditto," Tammy said

Going up to the window, Howard gave their orders adding his own of another chocolate milkshake.

As he received and paid for their orders, he carried them to the car and distributed them, then climbed into the car and headed home.

CHAPTER TWENTY-EIGHT

By seven A.M. the next day everyone was up and dressed as they got ready to face the issues of the day. Tina was excited with the possibility of finally being entered at school. Dorothy was hoping she would be enrolled in her class. Howard was ready to face his day as was Ella. Tammy, her heart beating with anticipation over the job she was certain God had for her. As soon as breakfast was over, each of them went their ways.

Tammy took the keys to Ella's car and she and Tina got in and headed for the school. (Dorothy had already left with Howard). The office was open when they entered so Tammy was able to get Tina registered in a few minutes. Tina was thrilled when she was told that she would be in the same class with Dorothy. As she left to go to her class, Tammy left to go to Motorola. She arrived there in ample time for her appointment as she parked the car and entered the building.

Walking up to the receptionist, she gave her name. "Oh, yes," the receptionist replied. "Right this way. The superintendent is waiting for you.."

Tammy entered the door she indicated. Roger Albain, the superintendent, stood to his feet to greet her, indicating a chair for her to be seated. "Good morning! I trust this is a day you have been looking forward to."

"Yes it is," Tammy replied. "I'm quite thrilled with the possibility of working for Motorola."

"Fine. Let's get right down to brass tacks then. If I am right, I believe your expertise is in auditing. Does that include a knowledge of bookkeeping?"

"Yes, it does. In fact, I was a bookkeeper before I became an auditor."

"That's fine! You'll fit right in here then. Now, I suppose you're interested in the financial end of the deal. Right?"

"Yes, sir."

"Okay. You will be on salary. We pay on the first and the fifteenth of each month. You will work forty hours a week and have two weeks vacation each year for the first five years.

After that, should you remain here, one week will be added to your vacation time every five years. How does that sound to you?"

'That part is fine." Tammy replied, "but I am also interested in the remuneration. I have a daughter to support and will have to rent or buy a house."

"Of course. Your salary to start will be two thousand dollars a month with raises every six months as you qualify. Paydays are the first and fifteenth of the month, unless it falls on a holiday. Then it would fall on the first workday prior to the regular payday. We also have an insurance plan, if you are interested in that, and an annuity plan that you can enroll in. You can enroll in that any time. Does that answer your questions?"

"Indeed it does!" Does this mean that I am hired? And when do I start?"

"Yes, it means you are hired and you can start Monday, if that is agreeable."

"It certainly is! And you have made me a very happy woman! Thank you." She rose from her chair, as he rose also.

"I forgot to mention that this will all be written in a contract. It will be printed and ready for you to sign when you come in Monday. Good-day and God bless you."

"Thank you."

Tammy turned and went out to the outer office. "I'll see you Monday morning," she said to the receptionist who sat at her desk.. Then went out to the car and headed home, her heart singing. When she drove into the driveway, she noted that Howard's car was there,too. Then both the girls came bounding out of the house when they heard her car drive in.

"You came just in time." Tina cried. "Did you get the job?"

Tammy and the Pharmacist

"Wait until I get inside and I can tell everyone at once."

"OK."

Howard and Ella were at the table. The two girls took their places, then Tammy sat down at the place laid for her and took a big breath.. "Well, I know you're all anxious to hear so I'll get right to it. I have a job! I start at 8 AM Monday morning. I'll be doing both auditing and bookkeeping. I'll be on salary payable on the first and fifteenth of the month, I'll get two weeks vacation every year. Um! What did I leave out?"

"Mom, you're teasing us," Tina cried. "How much are they going to pay you?"

"Oh, that! Well, my starting salary will be two thousand dollars a month!"

Howard let out a low whistle. "That's great! What a wonderful Lord we have."

"Oh, Tammy, I'm so glad for you!" Ella cried.

Dorothy and Tina were both ecstatic. "Now we can get a house and a car. " Tina said.

"Not so fast," Tammy replied. "They don't pay you in advance. You have to work first, but we can begin looking for something. It just might be that we will be living on the ranch if our plans work out to get one started. We have to wait until we see what God's plans are. We'll find out a lot about that when Robert gets here next week and we see what the church will be providing and what our part will be. They might have someone in the congregation that is already planning such a venture. We don't come in expecting to take over but cooperate in whatever God has planned. Isn't that right, Howard?"

"Yes, it certainly is. Now, I've got to get back to work and these girls to school. We'll see you two later and continue this conversation tonight."

After they left, Ella said, "I'm so happy for you. I know the Lord has worked this out for your good. Do you have anything special that you need to do this afternoon."

"Not really. I had pretty decent clothes for work at Macys so I won't need dresses right away. I'd like to wait to look at a car until Robert comes. He might be able to get me a real good deal.

Having only the money from the car he sold will keep me from spending rashly. I'm not even certain about looking for a house until I see the results from the meeting next Thursday night. If we find a place already built and we are asked to live there and oversee the children that would simplify things. If not, we just have to wait and see. Anyway, I think I'll just take it easy and follow the Lord's leading."

"I think you're being very wise. There's no need to rush. We're one big, happy family now so let's just take it one step at a time as the Lord leads." Ella replied.

"Thank you." Right now, if there isn't anything to do here, I guess I'll go to my room and take a short nap."

"Good idea. I think I will, too."

After dinner that evening, they gathered in the living room for family worship. Each of them brought their Bibles so they could follow the scriptures as Howard read them. As he opened his Bible, he said he thought it would be a good idea to continue reading in John. "I think we should read a whole book until it is finished and then go to the next one. We may need to notice the references in the margin referring us to the same scriptures in other books. We should take turns doing that so that we all become familiar with the entire Bible. How does that sound to you?"

"That sounds like a great idea to me." Tammy interjected. " It's a good way to learn the whole Bible. Many of the references point you to the Old Testament and many are prophecies that pertain to the present day and the 'soon coming' of Christ."

"Do you believe He's coming real soon? "Dorothy asked.

"Yes, I do. There's a scripture in Matthew where Jesus tells us if we see certain things happening we'll know the end is near." Tammy replied. "He likens it to when we see green leaves on a fig tree, we'll know spring is near."

"Let's open to the book of John. Let's see, where were we reading last? Did you mark your books? That might be a good idea."

"I have it!" Dorothy said. "May I start reading?"

"Yes," Howard replied, "you read until anyone has a question about a certain scripture or where there are references in the margin that we want to look up. Then someone else will go from there, Ok. Dorothy. Go ahead."

Dorothy began to read, "John 1:6 There was a man sent from God, whose name was John. The same came for a witness, to bear witness of the Light, that all men through him might believe. He was not that Light, but was sent to bear witness of that Light. That was the true Light, which lighteth every man that cometh into the world. I'd like to stop here and find out who this man was that was sent from God. "

"Good girl!" Howard exclaimed. "Tammy, can you help us here?"

"Certainly. This man, John, who was sent from God is a cousin of Jesus. He was six months older than Jesus and his birth was clothed in mystery just as Jesus' was, although he had an earthly father. Turn to Matthew 3:1-16 to see John the Baptist' ministry. Howard, why don't you read that part?"

"OK," he replied as he began to read. "In those days came John, the Baptist., preaching in the wilderness of Judea and saying, Repent ye: for the kingdom of heaven is at hand. For this is he that was spoken of by the prophet, Isaiah, saying THE VOICE OF ONE CRYING IN THE WILDERNESS, PREPARE YE THE WAY OF THE LORD. MAKE HIS PATHS STRAIGHT.(there are two scriptures here that we should look up but I suggest we read the rest of this chapter and then go back to these scriptures later). And the same John had his raiment of camel's hair, and a leathern girdle about his loins: and his meat was locusts and wild honey. Then went out to him Jerusalem, and all Judea, and all the region round about Jordan, and were baptized of him in Jordan, confessing their sins.."

At this point, Dorothy interrupted. "Could you tell us what 'baptism' is? Is it something we should do?"

Howard asked Tammy if she would answer that question.

"Yes," Tammy responded. "Christians ARE expected to be baptized as soon as there is an opportunity for them to do so. It is a witness to the world that you have been born again and accepted Jesus as your savior."

"Can we be baptized and where do we do it?" Ella asked.

"The church has a baptistery and baptism is offered every so often to those who have given their life to Jesus. It is a very solemn and impressive occasion.. Some churches that do not have a baptistery go to a river or lake and perform their baptisms there just like John the Baptist did. Even Jesus was baptized by John, as you will see later in this same chapter, as an example to us."

Howard continued to read, "But when he (John) saw many of the Pharisees and Sadducees come to his baptism, he said unto them, O generation of vipers, who hath warned *you* to flee from the wrath to come? Bring forth therefore fruits meet for repentance, and think not to say within yourselves, We have Abraham to our father; for I say unto you, that God is able of these stones to raise up children unto Abraham. And now also the axe is laid unto the root of the trees and, every tree that bringeth not forth good fruit is hewn down and cast into the fire."

"What were Pharisees and Sadducees? "Dorothy asked.

Tammy replied, "They were religious sects that were against Jesus."

"Howard continues, "I (John) indeed baptize you with water unto repentance; but he that cometh after me is mightier than I, whose shoes I am not worthy to bear: he shall baptize you with the Holy Ghost and with fire Whose fan is in his hand, and he will thoroughly purge his floor, and gather his wheat into the garner; but burn up the chaff with unquenchable fire.. " I really think we should wait until tomorrow night to finish this chapter. This really gives us much to chew on and digest! Tammy, do you have anything to add or explain about these scriptures? I confess I'm at a loss right now to figure it all out myself, let alone explain it to someone else."

"I'll try. First of all, John is talking about the religious sects of his day which, much like some sects today, stirred up trouble for the disciples and those followers who accepted Jesus as their Savior, much like some religions do today. They boasted that Abraham was their Father but I don't think they knew Abraham or what he believed. Then when John is referring to Jesus, it is how he will clean house, so to speak, and set his house in order. When we finish this chapter tomorrow, we will see that Jesus practices what he preaches by being baptized himself by John."

"Then shall we bow to him in prayer?" Howard asked.

Each one bowed by their seat and spoke out in prayer as they were led by the spirit..

Tina prayed first. "Thank you, Father, for the privilege of reading your Word. How precious it is to each of us. Teach us thy will and thy way as we endeavor to learn thy ways."

Dorothy followed. "Thank you, Jesus, for thy word. Help us to understand it. Thank you so much for hearing and answering prayer. Amen."

Ella, too, Lifted her heart in prayer. "Thank you, Father , for teaching our children to pray. It is a delight to us to hear them talk to thee, May we ever be an example to them and to our friends and neighbors, that they come to know you, also, as their savior. Thank you for blessing Tammy with a job. She is such a blessing to us. Bless her, Lord, real good."

Tammy, her voice choked with emotion, began to pray "Thank you, blessed Jesus, for these dear friends who have come to our rescue when we were in despair. Help us to be a witness to others who need to know you, too. Bless Iris and her husband and Howard's partner, Tom. They all need you, Lord. Amen.

Howard closed the prayer with his own petition. " I am of all men, most blessed. To have a family and friends who know you as Savior and Lord is wonderful! Help us to remember to keep your name before our friends and neighbors that they might come to see how you have blessed us and want to come to know you also. Help us to remember to invite Valerie and David over. We don't know yet whether they know you or not but bless our efforts to win them if they don't. Lead and guide us as we talk to others at church about the possibility of obtaining land for the ranch or whatever you have in mind for homeless children. Show us where you want it to be. We praise and thank you for all that you are doing that your kingdom might flourish here. Amen."

They rose to their feet and Howard said to Ella. "Do you think we could have Valerie and David over for a barbecue tomorrow? "

"Yes, I think that would be a great idea! Why don't you go call them now?"

"Ok, I'll do that!" He went to get his briefcase and pulled the address and telephone number from it. Going to the phone, he lifted the receiver and dialed their number.

David answered the phone. "Hello?"

"David, this is Howard Peters. How are you?"

"I'm fine. How are you? I was just telling Valerie that we hadn't heard from you and that maybe we ought to call you and see how you were."

"Well, we've had a very busy time. We've brought Tammy and her daughter out here. Tammy has got a job and will be living here but we were wondering if you and Valerie might be able to come over tomorrow for that barbecue we were talking about."

"Wow! I don't know if Valerie has anything planned. Just a moment. I'll ask her....... She is delighted. We've been anxious to see you folks. What can we bring? And what time do you want us to come?"

"How about five o'clock. It will be a little cooler that time of day., You don't need to bring anything, just yourselves."

"That sounds fine to me. We'll see you then. I'm really looking forward to it!"

"OK, we'll see you then. 'Bye."

"Howard turned to Ella. I told him five o'clock. That way, if we have to get anything from the store, we'll have time. OK?"

"Yes" she replied. "There are some things we'll need.

"What do you intend to barbecue?"

"I think chicken would be good. I know it would be tender. Some meats can be tough and everybody likes chicken."

"You're right. We can buy it already cut up. Any idea what you'd like for dessert?"

"You know me." Howard replied. "Any kind of pie with a scoop of ice cream on top would suit me fine."

"How about a big salad and potato chips to go with it?"

And maybe a pan of baked beans?" Ella asked.

"Sounds good to me."

"OK I guess I'll get started on those pies then. We should have at least two. How about a pumpkin pie for one and maybe an apple for the other?"

Tammy and the Pharmacist

"Fine, but we'd better get some Cool Whip for the pumpkin. You wouldn't want ice cream on that, would you?' Howard asked.

"We'll get some to be sure. We can always use it. Especially with two hungry girls to feed." With that settled, each went to do their own thing. Ella went to the kitchen to start on her pies. Tammy went to see if she could help her.

Ella said, "You can peel the apples while I do the pumpkin, if you'd like." As the two of them worked together they talked of the thing that was uppermost in their hearts, the ranch they hoped to build for homeless boys and girls and the prospect of Robert Green coming to help in the project.

"This Robert Green, what is he like?" Ella asked.

"You mean is he tall, dark and handsome, "Tammy laughed.

"Well, that, too, but how old is he, is he or has he been married? Things like that.

"Hmmmn. I'll have to think on that. I don't think he's ever been married. At least he isn't now. How old is he? Oh, I'd say around thirty-five or thirty-eight. He's good-looking; at least I think so. He has dark brown curly hair that's always falling over his eyes which are a very dark brown. He's about six foot tall, slender and willowy. And, best of all, he's a Christian."

"Uh- huh! No wonder you're so anxious to have him come out here."

"Now, Ella, don't you go getting ideas in your head and for goodness sake, don't let the girls hear you. He's just a friend."

'"All right. I won't tease you anymore but I'll be praying that the Lord will work it out if that's his will!"

"Anything that's the Lord's will is OK with me. We'll just let the Lord have his way. I have the apples all done. Do you have a pie crust ready for them?"

"Yes, it's right here. Do you want to put them in and put the sugar and cinnamon on them?"

"Sure."

"I'll put the top crust on after I finish this pumpkin pie. Do you want to go sit down for awhile? I'll come in as soon as I get them in the oven."

"OK. I'll be in the living room."

Ella didn't tease Tammy any more but she did pray about it as she said she would. She thought it would make a very well rounded finish (or beginning, according to how you looked at it) for two very wonderful people.

CHAPTER TWENTY-NINE

Saturday morning dawned a bright sunny morning as Ella prepared to go shopping for the barbecue that evening. Armed with her purse and a shopping list, she got her car keys and prepared to buy the things they had talked about last night. She had laid out the things the rest of the family would need for breakfast and hurried out to her car. She wanted to get her shopping done and get back before the heat of the day. She was glad they'd got the pies done last night. She would still have to bake the beans but they could simmer at a lower heat. Anyway she could put the air -conditioning on for awhile. She thought she ought to ask Iris and George over, too, for tonight.

Just as she got in her car, she saw Iris on the porch and called to her. "H! Iris. We're having a barbecue tonight at 5 P.M. Want to come over and join us?"

Iris, "Sure, what's the occasion?"

"Nothing special. Just wanted to get some friends together. I don't think you've had a chance to meet Tammy and her daughter and another couple Howard met on the plane to New York. You'll enjoy all of them, I'm sure."

"Okay, what can I bring? "

"You don't have to bring anything. Just come."

'"Nope. I don't contribute, I don't come."

"Okay, " laughing. "How about a casserole of baked beans?"

""That I will do. See you tonight."

Ella went on her way singing. "Trust and obey, for there's no other way, to be happy in Jesus but to trust and obey.".

Tammy and the Pharmacist

When she got back from her shopping, Tammy and the girls were up and had breakfasted. The kitchen was spic and span . They all ganged up on Ella. " Where have you been?" they cried.

"Grocery shopping," Ella said.

"Howard said he was going down to the pharmacy for a few hours. He says they get most of their business in the morning. He's going to try to get Tom to come to the barbecue." Tammy said. "Does Tom have a wife or a girl friend?"

"I really don't know. I'll be surprised if he comes."

"I talked to Iris and asked her and George to come over.

She said she wouldn't come unless she brought something so I told her to bring a casserole of baked beans. You'll like her and George. We're trying to get them interested in coming to church, too."

"Does anybody play an instrument?" Tammy asked. "We could have an old-fashioned gospel sing."

"I believe Tom plays a guitar. Maybe that would be an incentive to get him to come. I'll call and ask him."

"Great! Tammy said. "I have an Omni-chord that I brought with me."

"You know," Ella said, "I think Iris said George plays a harmonica." I'll call her and find out about that, too."

"Wow! This sounds like it will be a real fun evening!"

The girls chorused.

Ella had put her groceries away as they talked. Now she sat down with the phone to make her phone calls. She dialed the phone at the pharmacy. Tom answered. "Hi, Tom, just the guy I wanted to talk to. If I remember right, you play a guitar, don't you?"

"Why, yes, I do. "

"Well, would you bring it along tonight? We're planning on having a music group and a sing-a-long. Also, do you have a girl-friend you'd like to bring??"

"Wow, Ella, I haven't played with a group for a long time. But, by golly, I can try. And yes. I do have a girl friend.

I'll call her and see if she'll come with me. And thanks for asking me. It sounds like fun. What time did you say?"

"Five o'clock. It's a barbecue and all you have to bring is your girl, your guitar and yourself!"

"Hot darn! We'll be there."

"Okay! Now can I talk to Howard a minute?"

"Sure. I'll call him."

"Hello"

"Hi, it's Ella. I just talked to Tom. He's bringing his guitar, his girl and an appetite! We're going to have a sing-a-long."

"Wow! You're one fast worker. Wonderful!" See you at noon."

Next Ella called Iris. Luckily, George answered the phone. "Hi, George, it's Ella. Do you still have your harmonica? We want to have a sing-a-long tonight. You do"? Will you bring it with you? Oh, thanks. See you later then."

She called to Tammy, "You better get your Omni chord tuned up! We're having a sing-a-long tonight!"

Tammy came out into the kitchen. "You're one fast worker," she said. "So. Who all will be playing?"

"Tom is bringing his guitar, his girl and an appetite and thrilled to be playing. Also, George will be playing his harmonica. You will be playing your Omni Chord.... Do you know the song, Prayer is the Key to Heaven?"

"Yes, I do. What about other songs? "Tammy asked.

"Well, since we want to tread softly here, I think we should use old familiar songs like 'Put on your old gray bonnet; Mr. Sandman, bring me a dream; etc. We'll have to print up a song sheet. Could you do that on the computer?"

"Sure," Tammy replied. "You just write them down, I probably know most of them. I'll sort of use the old time songs first and then gradually add some hymns and church songs. Okay?"

"Fine," Ella replied. "The computer is in Howard's den. I'm sure he won't mind you using it."

"OK. Write your list down and I'll print them up. How many copies do you think we'll need?"

"I'd say at least twenty-five. Maybe some of the neighbors will hear and want to come join in."

"Will do!" Tammy replied

"Here's the list. Put then in whatever order you think they should go. Mr. Sandman, Bring Me a Dream; Put on Your Old Gray Bonnet; Old MacDonald, Peace in the Valley, Que Sera, Sera; Blue Skies, Amazing Grace, Give Me that Old Time Religion; He's Got the Whole World in His Hands; I Believe. Is that enough? Print the words to your solo' Prayer is the Key to Heaven.' People can take the song sheets home with them, too."

"I think so. Do you want the words printed as well as the titles?"

"Oh, yes! Some people wouldn't know the words to the church songs and some may not know the other old-time songs"

" Can I take your song-book along? I may not remember all the words either." Ella handed her the book and she left to sort the songs out and print them up in the right order."

About an hour later, Howard came home to find every-body busy, Tammy was just finishing up the printing of the song list for the evening. Ella was finishing the salad she was making. The girls were working a jigsaw puzzle. It was a busy household. "I haven't seen so much activity in this house for a long time," he said.

"I guess everybody will have to make themselves a sandwich," Ella said. "We don't have time to cook right now. We're too busy getting ready for tonight. Is Tom going to take off early?"

"Yes, I said we'd leave a note on the door in case some one had to have a prescription in a hurry. I put our phone number on it. I can always run down and take care of it. Tom is real excited about the barbecue and the sing-a-long."

"You know, " Ella replied. "I 'm sure Jesus is behind this barbecue, too!" Just then Tammy walked out with the song sheets she had printed.

Howard took one to look at it. "This is great! You know, we should have asked the pastor and his wife to come, too."

"We can always have another one," Ella said. "I wouldn't be surprised if this wouldn't catch on and spread.. If anyone wants a sandwich, help your self. I'm going to take a snooze so I'll have some energy to finish fixing dinner tonight. You're going to do the barbecuing, aren't you?" She asked Howard.

"Yes! I sure will. Go take your snooze. We'll manage just fine."

CHAPTER THIRTY

At four o'clock, Ella arose and got ready for the final touches to the barbecue. They had placed a long folding table on the lanai and the girls were arranging stacks of paper plates and dinnerware. Howard was arranging chairs and had the barbecue set up ready to go.

Iris and George came over to see if they could help.

"Everything is pretty much under control but do you happen to have a microphone?" Howard asked.

"No. I never had occasion to use one." George replied.

"Hmm. I wonder if Tom might have one. He used to play with a group. I'll ask him when he gets here. He doesn't live very far from here and could go get it."

Tammy spoke up, "I think we can get along without it. It would be nice to have but not absolutely necessary."

"Here comes Tom and his friend now. You haven't met them yet, have you?"

"No, I haven't. Nor Iris and George either."

"Golly, sorry about that," Howard said. "Iris and George, meet Tammy and her daughter, Tina, our house guests from New York."

Iris grabbed Tammy and hugged her. "I'm so glad to meet both of you. Ella told us about you before you came. I know Dorothy is happy to have you here, Tina, and so are we."

Just then Tom and his girl friend came up. Tom introduced her. " Hi! This is my friend, Lucy."

"Lucy, we're so happy to have you. Let me introduce you to the others. This is Iris, our neighbor and her husband, George." Howard responded. Iris grabbed Lucy and hugged her. George shook her hand.

Just then Valerie and David arrived. " Hello, you two!

Glad we finally got together. Wait just a minute until I get the rest of the gang so we can make all our introductions at once."

Howard said., then called, "Ella, can you come out here a minute? Our guests are all here."

Ella and Dorothy came out, Ella brushing her hair back from her face. "Sorry," she said. "I just had a few last minute things to do."

Howard took her hand and drew her over to Valerie and David. "This is my wife, Ella." Ella welcomed Valerie with a hug and shook hands with David. Then turned to Tammy and Tina and Dorothy. "These are our house guests, Tammy and her daughter, Tina. This is our daughter, Dorothy. We hope you'll all have a good time tonight and that we'll see a lot more of each other. Tom is Howard's partner at the pharmacy and this is his girlfriend, Lucy. Now I'd better get that chicken out here so Howard can get it on the grill."

Howard spoke to Tom. " Tammy wants to know if you have a portable microphone?"

"Yeah, I got one."

"Would it take you very long to run get it?"

"No more'n five minutes. It's in the trunk of the car."

Howard, giving Tom a big hug. "You sure are full of surprises tonight! Guess I'd better get over there and get that chicken going"

The other guests sat around in a circle, renewing acquaintances and learning more about their new friends. It was a very congenial bunch. Tammy circulated, getting acquainted with each one. Tom went out to his car to get his microphone. He looked for an outlet to plug it into. Howard and Ella had strung lights for later on when they had the Sing-a-long. He was able to plug it in right where it would be needed the most. Soon, Howard called out, "Chicken's done! Shall we all stand up to give thanks. Tammy, will you ask the blessing?"

"Certainly. Shall we bow our heads? Dear Heavenly Father, we come to you to thank you for this lovely gathering of people. We ask you to bless the food we are about to partake and to bless our fellowship this evening. Thank you for hearing us pray. Amen"

Tammy and the Pharmacist

"OK, everybody, find a place and dig in. I hope you're all hungry." With that, everyone found a seat as Howard placed a huge platter of chicken on the table. He and Ella sat at the head of the table, helping to pass the drinks and food. Soon everyone was quiet, their mouths too full of good things to waste time on words. When their tummies were satisfied they began to talk again.

"What a meal" Tom said. "I'm so stuffed it's a good thing I have to play rather than sing,"

"Me. Too." Said George.

"Hmm," Howard spoke up, "Maybe we ought to chase everybody around the block "

"No way," said David. "I'll just stand up and stretch a few times."

"Me, too." The rest echoed. So saying, they stood up and stretched a bit while Ella and Dorothy put the empty plates in the trash can and carried the balance of the meal to put it in the refrigerator.

"When Ella came out, she said, "I notice most of you didn't eat any pie. After the Sing-a-long you might want a piece before you go home. OK?"

"Tammy", Howard said. "We'll turn the rest over to you."

"OK, Tom and George, if you'll bring your chairs over here, we'll get set-up. Howard, will you bring me a chair, too, please?" As the three of them got settled in their place she said to the rest. You'll notice that there is a song sheet at each place and that the songs are numbered according the page it's on in my book. If you have a certain song that you'd like to sing, just sing out the name and number of the song and we'll endeavor to play it. We've never played together before so please be patient with us. How about it fellas? Should we heist a tune first. How about The Old Gray Mare?"

Tammy sat down and adjusted her book on her music stand. Turning to the page she had indicated, she began to strum her Omnichord. Catching on, the two men began to play; Tom on the guitar and George on the harmonica.

Then Tammy began to sing, "Oh, the old gray mare, she ain't what she used to be, ain't what she used to be, ain't what she used to be. The old gray mare ain't what she used to be many long years ago."

"Hey, that's great!" David called. "How about Old MacDonald had a farm. P. 121."

"Ok. Here we go!"

"Old McDonald had a farm. E-I-E-I-O
And on this farm he had a duck. E-I-E-I-O
With a quack-quack here, and a quack-quack there.
Here a quack, there a quack
Ev'rywhere a quack, quack.
Old Mc Donald had a farm. E-I-E-I-O.
And on this farm he had a cow. E-I-E-I-O,
With a moo-moo here, and a moo-moo there
Here a moo, there a moo
Ev'rywhere a moo, moo
Old Mc Donald had a farm, E-I-E-I-O!
And on this farm he had a pig,E-I-E-I-O
With an oink-oink here, and an oink-oink there
Here an oink, there an oink
Ev'rywhere an oink, oink E-I-E-I-O
Old McDonald had a farm E-I-E-I-O
And on this farm he had a cat E-I-E-I-O
With a me-ow here and a me-ow there
Here a me-ow, there a me-ow
Ev'ry where a me-ow, me-ow
Old Mc Donald had a farm E-I-E-I-O!!!!

By now, everybody was laughing so hard they could hardly sing. "How about you singing a solo now? "Howard called.

"Okay" Tammy replied. "This is called 'Faith Unlocks the Door."

"Prayer is the Key to Heaven but
Faith unlocks the door.
Words are so easily spoken but prayer without Faith
Is like a boat without an oar.

Cho: Have faith, when you speak to the Master,
       That's all He asks you for,
       YES, prayer is the key to Heaven,
       But FAITH UNLOCKS THE DOOR!"

How many times have you prayed
For something big or small?
How long did you have to wait,
Or did the answer come at all?

Cho:　Have Faith when you speak to the Master,
That's all he asks you for.
Yes, Prayer is the Key to Heaven
But FAITH UNLOCKS THE Door!"

There was a lot of hand-clapping when Tammy finished and a lot of thoughtful expressions on some of the faces.

"What shall we sing next?" she asked.
"How about Blue Skies; page 24? Dorothy asked.
Tammy turned over to that song in her book and strummed a few notes, then began to sing as the group joined in.
"Blue skies, smiling at me,
Nothing but blue skies do I see.
Blue birds singing a song,
Nothing but blue birds all day long
Never saw the sun shining so bright,
Never saw things going so right!
Noticing the days hurrying by,
When you're in love
My how they fly!
Blue days, all of them gone,
Nothing but Blue Skies from now on!"

"That's me" Tina cried. "I'm in love with Arizona!"

How about 'He's Got the Whole World in His Hands, p61?"
"OK, Here we go" responded Tammy.
"He's got the whole wide world in His hands,
He's got the whole wide world in His hands,
He's got the whole wide world in His hands,
He's got the whole world in His Hands.

He's got the tiny little baby in His hands'
He's got the tiny little baby in His hands,
He's got the tiny little baby in His hands,
He's got the whole world in His hands.

He's got you and me, brother in His hands
He's got you and me, brother in His hands
He' got you and me, brother in His hands
He's got the whole world in His hands."

"Lets have one more song before we get at those pies. Howard, do you have a song you'd like us to sing?"
"Yes. I do. How about 'Peace in the Valley, P.126?"

Tammy turned to that page in the book and began to strum the tune. Then as the others joined in, they began to sing,
"I am tired and weary but I must toil on,
Till the Lord comes to call me away.
Where the morning is bright
And the Lamb is the light, and the night
Is as fair as the day.
There'll be Peace in the Valley for me some day,
There'll be Peace in the Valley for Me, I pray.
No more sorrow and sadness or trouble will be,
But there'll be Peace in the Valley for Me."

There was much more clapping of hands and a few tears as the group began to break up. Ella brought out the pies and a big pot of coffee as well as carbonated drinks for those who preferred them. No one left but all gathered around the table as they partook of the desserts. In fact, they seemed reluctant to go. Finally, as they began to leave they came up to Howard and expressed how much they had enjoyed them selves. David said, "I think you ought to keep that trio together. They really sounded good. Are you folks going to church in the morning?"
"Yes, we wouldn't think of missing. It's the high-light of our week."

"Well, look for Valerie and me. I'm sure I know where your church is. It's the biggest one in Phoenix. Right?"

"Yes, it is."

"Well, we'll see you there tomorrow morning. OK?"

"Great! We'll be looking for you. You might make plans to come Thursday night, too. We're looking into getting land for a ranch for homeless boys and girls. I think you'd find it interesting."

"Great, we'll do that. What time is it?"

"7:30. Robert Warren, a friend of Tammy's, is flying out for the meeting and will stay until Sunday. He's interested in this, too, and plans to move out here. We're pretty excited about it."

"Okay, we'll see you tomorrow morning then. 'Bye"

CHAPTER THIRTY-ONE

Sunday morning found not only Howard and all his family at church but, surprise, surprise there were Tom and Lucy as well as David and Valerie, *and* George and Iris! Howard could hardly contain his joy as he went around introducing them to the Pastor and other members he had come to know. The Pastor was cordial to all of them inviting them to sit near the front so they could be formally introduced to the congregation. Later, the Pastor told of the special meeting to be held on Thursday evening to discuss plans for finding a site for a possible ranch for homeless boys and girls. He also mentioned that Robert Warren would be there to talk about the plans. He invited everyone interested in such a plan to be in attendance that night. There was quite a stir of interest. The Pastor thought they might possibly have to use the main auditorium for that meeting.

After the morning service was over, Howard and his friends met in front of the church where they all decided to go somewhere and eat dinner together. He told them of the café where they had eaten the Sunday before so they all decided to go there, too. Howard was glad because he knew there would be quite a contingent of church people and he wanted to cement the friendships that had been started. As before, they had the waitress push the tables together so everyone who wished to, could sit together. There was an animated buzz of conversation. After the dinner, each went their own ways but many pledged to be there on Thursday night. After hearing of the barbecue and Sing Along Saturday night, many were interested in having such an occasion themselves. Looked like the new trio and their song leader were going to be right busy!"

CHAPTER THIRTY-TWO

Monday morning was another new beginning for Tammy as she began her new job at Motorola. Dressed in a smart navy blue suit, she exuded confidence. She was welcomed by the receptionist in the outer office and taken to the office where she would be working.. The superintendent who had hired her was there to welcome her and show her what her job would consist of. Evidently she would be responsible for this office and would report directly to him. A little shaken by this revelation, she was nevertheless confident of her ability to handle the job. After he had shown her the ropes, he went to his own office leaving her free to work on her own. This was heady stuff.

Getting her computer set up and locating the books she would be working with, she looked through the in-box on her desk and began to enter the accounts on the computer. Knowing how computers can sometimes get jinxed, she moved to save every item and made printouts of valuable information.

Noon was there before she realized it. The receptionist stuck her head in the door. "Time for lunch, do you want to go to the cafeteria?"

"Oh, yes, may I go with you?"

"Yes, that's why I stopped."

"Great. I didn't know where the cafeteria was." Taking her purse, she closed her door and went with the receptionist.. "I'm sorry, but I didn't get your name."

"My name is Margaret. And yours is Tammy. Right?"

"Yes. I'm glad to get to know you."

"I know. The first day is always a little scary. If you need any help, just let me know."

"Thank you, Margaret. That's good to know. I believe we have an hour for lunch. Is that right?"

"Yes, it is. And there is also a fifteen minute break in the morning and one in the afternoon."

"Great! I think I'll be able to get along fine but I value your friendship. Is this the cafeteria?"

"Yes. Would you like to sit together?"

"Of course. Let's get our trays and find a seat. I don't want to be late getting back." They got in line, filled their trays and found a table. "I'm used to returning thanks. Do you mind?"

"No, not at all." She bowed her head as Tammy prayed, then resumed her questions as they began to eat.

"Where are you from?"

"I had been living in New York City until a week or so ago but I grew up in Arizona so it's like coming home."

"That's wonderful. Are you married?"

" No, my husband was killed in a train crash a year ago. I have a twelve-year old daughter. I just entered her in school Friday morning before I came here. We're staying with friends until I get a couple of pay-days under my belt."

"Golly! Sounds like a fairy-tale."

"Believe me, it's no fairy-tale. But I do have a wonderful Lord who takes care of us. If you don't mind, I believe I'll head on back. I have so much to do that I want to use every spare minute to get everything in order, especially the computer. I'll see you later. OK?"

"Oh, sure. I'll be going back real soon myself."

"OK, see you there." Tammy hurried back to her office and set to work organizing the computer, checking the files and her in/out basket to see what needed to be done yet that day. At 3:15 she took time out to go to the bathroom as she hadn't taken time at lunch. By five o'clock she had everything pretty well set-up and the computer was working like a charm. She closed her desk, turned the computer off, shut and locked the files and was ready to leave when the Superintendent looked in to see how she was doing."

Tammy and the Pharmacist

"Just fine, Mr. Albain" she said. "I have everything entered in the computer, the files are in order and everything is up to date in my in/out basket. Do you have any instructions you wished to give me?"

"No. Just wanted to see if you needed any help but I can see you don't. Should you need anything at all, just knock on my door. It will always be open to you."

"Thank you. I'll remember that."

"Good-night then."

"Good-night." Tammy locked her door, took her purse and walked out, breathing a sigh of relief that her first day was over.

When she walked in the door at Ella's, both the girls came running to see how her day had been.

"Just great", she said, "but you'll have to wait until dinner to hear the details. I'm just too tired to tell it more than once. So Ella, did Iris come over? How did she like the service yesterday?"

"Yes, she came over and said both she and George had enjoyed the barbecue so very much and they loved the morning service. Howard is in Seventh Heaven!"

"He sure is!" Howard said as he stepped in the door.

"You'd never know the difference in Tom today. All he could talk about is the barbecue and your little band. A lot of people want the three of you to play more. And both he and Lucy loved the church and plan on coming all the time. I think there's going to be some wedding bells there!"

"Wow!" They all chorused.

"So. Mom, can you tell us about your day now that Howard is home?" Tina asked.

"Yes, I became acquainted with the receptionist who sits in the outer office and we went to lunch together in the cafeteria. Her name is Margaret but she sure can ask a lot of questions.. I didn't think we were going to have time to eat so I sort of had to suggest that we get our trays and find a seat so we could eat our lunch. I needed to get back as early as I could, I had to program everything into the computer and make back-ups just in case we'd have a glitch. I finally got everything organized just before 5 o'clock and was locking the files and everything up when Mr. Albain, the Superintendent stuck his head in the door. He said if I needed anything to just knock on his door. He's awfully nice. Anyway, I closed up my office and headed for home. Thank you so much, Ella, for the use of your car. I don't know what I'd do without it."

CHAPTER THIRTY-THREE

Tuesday and Wednesday went by without incident and the Peter's household settled down to a normal routine. Ella breathed a sigh of relief. They still had their family worship in the evening and it, too, was a time of refreshing as they learned more about John the Baptist and his relationship with Jesus. Let's listen in as Tina reads the scripture from Matthew 3:13.

Tina: "Then cometh Jesus from Galilee to Jordan unto John, to be baptized of him. But John forbad him, saying I have need to be baptized of thee, and comest thou to me? And Jesus answering said, Suffer it to be so now; for thus it becometh us to fulfill all righteousness. Then he (John) suffered him. And Jesus, when he was baptized, went up straightway out of the water; and, lo, the heavens were opened unto him, and he saw the Spirit of God descending like a dove, and lighting upon him; And lo a voice from heaven, saying, This is my beloved Son, in whom I am well pleased." I was eight years old when I was baptized and I've never been sorry. If Jesus thinks it's that important, then so do I."

"Daddy," Dorothy asked. "Can we ask Pastor to have a baptism soon so we can be baptized? Maybe all those people who were here Saturday night might want to be baptized, too."

"Tell you what, let's pray about it and maybe all the others will accept Jesus as their Savior and we can have one big Baptism. OK?' As they assented, he then said, "Let us kneel down then and pray about all these things."

They knelt and Dorothy led out in prayer. "Dear Jesus, we're so happy we've come to know you and we want to follow in every way you lead us. Thank you for showing us the way. Help all these people we've been praying for to find you, too. We love you so very much. Amen."

Ella followed.," Dear Heavenly Father, we can't thank you enough for the way you have led us. I really think that barbecue was part of your plan. Six new people came to church because of it. We pray that every one of them will come to know you as Savior and Lord. Please guide us as we attempt to find property for the ranch that we feel is your leading. Give us wisdom in all that we do that we not get ahead of your Holy Spirit but learn to follow his leading. In the precious and Holy name of Jesus, we ask it."

"Heavenly Father," prayed Tammy, "We come before you tonight with hearts filled with jubilant praise. How blest we are to know you! Thank you again for the wonderful job you have given me. I pray for Margaret that she may come to know you as her Savior, too. And, as Ella has prayed give us wisdom to work your will in all that we do. Amen"

"Dear Jesus" Tina prayed. "We give you praise and thanksgiving tonight. How we love you! We pray you will open the door to all those who want or need Baptism without us having to say a word. We will just wait for you. In your precious name we ask it. Amen."

Howard took up the prayer, "Our precious Savior: we are filled with adoration tonight as we hear our loved ones lifting their hearts to you. How precious is our association with you. We still can't thank you enough for sending Tammy to bring me to you. Praise your name! And not only me, but our household, our neighbors and our friends. We pray that every one of these friends and others may come to accept you as Savior and Lord and that they, too, will obey you in baptism. Guide us as we walk this way, that we may have the leading of the Holy Spirit so that what we do will be according to your will and will bear much fruit for Thee. In your Holy and precious name we pray. Amen"

CHAPTER THIRTY-FOUR

Thursday was upon them before they knew it and Robert was on his way. Howard planned on meeting his plane and taking him to the motel he had reservations for. When the plane arrived, Howard met him with a big hug and waited while he claimed his luggage. Then took him to his motel. Robert registered, then Howard took him to an agency where he could rent a car. "You're coming home with me," Howard said. "Ella has a big dinner planned so you follow me, then you'll know where we live and can come over whenever you wish and, of course, the big meeting is tonight so we'll all go together. Ok?"

"Whatever you say, I sort of freshened up a bit on the plane because I figured we'd be pressed for time. How is Tammy doing?"

"She's doing just fine. I'll let her tell you herself about her job. We had a big barbecue last Saturday night and Tammy led a sing-a-long. Six people besides our family came to church on Sunday morning as a result. It's been fantastic."

"I can't wait to see them all. We've sure missed Tammy. I didn't know her daughter before Tammy brought her down to come here with her. Is anything special planned for Saturday? I'd like to take Tammy out. I thought we might be able to travel around the countryside and see what the lay of the land looks like."

"No, we don't have anything special for Saturday. We sort of thought you both might like to spend some time together."

"That's great!"

"Ok, you follow me. It's not far."

They both got in their cars and drove off.

When they reached Howard's house, he drove in and Robert followed, parking behind him. Howard thought they would probably need both cars as Iris and George might go with them.

Ella came out to meet them. "Welcome" she said,

We've been looking forward to your visit. The girls should be home a little after two-thirty. Tammy works until five, so she won't be home until about five thirty. We'll have dinner right away then as we'll all want to get to the church early. Our neighbors may go with us. C'mon in and make yourself at home."

"What a nice place you have," Robert exclaimed. I think I like Arizona already! It's so nice and warm here. New York is very cold already. I'm glad Tammy got a job so soon. Our Lord sure does take good care of us, doesn't he?"

"Yes, he does! " Ella asked "Would you like a soft drink or some iced tea, or would you prefer a cup of coffee?"

"Iced tea would be nice. Something sure smells good. What are you cooking?"

"A favorite of mine," she said as she brought him the iced tea, "it's called sweet and sour meat balls. Has pineapple, green peppers with soy sauce and brown sugar among other things and it is served over rice."

"Mmm, you're making my mouth water. I'm used to fast food places and it doesn't taste anything like home cooking."

"Tammy's a pretty good cook. She helps me sometimes."

"That,s good to know." (Ella grinned, score one, she thought.)

"Robert, would you like to come in the living room a while? You can even snooze a bit if you feel like it. ."Howard asked.

"Sure. I'll come in the living room but I don't feel like snoozing. I did a lot of that on the plane."

"Whatever you like is all right with me. How about television. We have a good Christian channel out here."

'That sounds great! I'd like to listen to that!"

"Okay, bring your tea and we'll go listen."

They hadn't listened very long when the girls came bounding in, "Hi, Robert, Tina said, "This is my friend, Dorothy. She's Howard and Ella's daughter and we're sisters now."

"Hey, that's great! Glad to meet you, Dorothy. I understand you have become a Christian, too."

"Oh, yes, I love Jesus and we're all going to be baptized as soon as they have a baptism at church."

"Mom should be home soon, Jesus gave her a great new job. We'll let her tell you about it. She wouldn't like it if we did it."

"That's all right. We'll wait for her to tell it."

"But I think we could tell about the barbecue can't we, Daddy?"

"Sure"

"Well, there was this couple that lives in Scottsdale. Daddy had met his wife on the plane and Daddy talked to him on the phone but never met him so we wanted to have them over for a barbecue. Then Mom asked Iris and George next door. And then she asked Tom, Daddy's partner to bring his girl. Okay Tina, you continue.'

"Well, she remembered Tom used to play the guitar, He said he still did and would bring it. Then Ella called to ask George if he still had his harmonica and would he bring it. He said yes...Mom had brought her omnichord, so we had a band, then Mom led the singing and we had a Sing-a-long. Everybody had a ball. And the whole bunch came to church on Sunday morning and everybody wants us to have more Sing-a-Longs."

"Wow! That's great! Did you have all fun songs?"

"Oh, no. We had some Christian songs, too. Mom sang a solo called Prayer Is the Key to Heaven. Some people were wiping tears out of their eyes."

"I sure wish I could have been here. Maybe we can have one the next time I come out."

"Well, you're just going to have to move out here like we did."

"I'm thinking real strong about it. I think tomorrow I'll canvass the automobile agencies and see if there is an opening.

If there is, I just might come out sooner than I thought. You might agree in prayer with me as I want the Lord to have his way in whatever I do."

"We'll do that," Howard replied and the others agreed as well as Ella, who had just come in.

Tammy and the Pharmacist

"Tammy will be here most any minute," she said. "If you'd like to wash up for dinner it will be on the table as soon as she gets here." They all made a mad scramble for the bathrooms, then assembled in the kitchen to wait for Tammy.

They didn't have to wait long till they heard the car parking behind the others. The others hung back giving Robert a chance to greet her first. He grabbed her and gave her a big hug. Flustered, her face flushed red; it was so unexpected. "Hi," she said, "I didn't realize you'd be here already."

"Yep," he said, "and I'm thinking about moving out here, too."

"Oh, that's wonderful,"

"And tomorrow while you're at work, I'm going to go around to the auto agencies and see what I can find in the way of a job. What do you think of that?"

"Well, you're just going to have to slow down a little bit and let me catch my breath. Things have been moving so fast around here that I can hardly keep up. I suppose the girls have already told you about the barbecue?"

"Yes, and I think it's fantastic. I know you're tired right now and Ella has dinner ready but I want to hear about your job, also. The girls said they didn't dare tell that!"

"They're right! Just wait until you hear. Maybe we can talk while we eat. That meeting tonight is at 7:30 so we have to hurry. The pastor told the congregation that you would be there tonight. Looks like your some sort of a celebrity here already."

Just then, Ella said dinner was ready and everyone sat down. She had placed Robert next to Tammy so they could talk.

Howard asked the blessing, "Thank you, Lord, for the food we're about to eat. Thank you for giving Robert a safe trip. Please be in the meeting tonight that we may do your will and not insist on having our own way. For thy glory, we ask it. Amen."

"I'm not going to ask you to tell me about your job right now so you can eat but maybe you could ride to the meeting in my car and you can tell me on the way. OK?"

"Sure, that'll be fine. I think it's important that we get there as early as possible."

Everyone stopped talking and concentrated on finishing their meal. As soon as they were done, they all pitched in and helped rid the table and put things in the dishwasher as Ella put the leftovers in the refrigerator.

"OK, said Howard," let's roll. You girls can ride with Ella and me." They all went out to get into their cars and were soon on their way.

When they got to the church, there was already quite a few people there. Pastor Bob was there to greet them and suggested they take seats up in front and asked if Howard, Tammy and Robert would take seats on the platform along with some of the board members who were already there. The church was fast filling up. Pastor Bob walked up to the podium as the board had asked him to chair the meeting. Taking a seat , he waited for those who were still coming in the door. At 7:30 sharp, he rose to open the service. "Shall we sing, Have Thine Own Way, Lord, before we pray. Tammy, would you lead us?"

Tammy rose and stepped to the podium. The keyboard player did a prelude, then Tammy began to sing as the congregation followed:

'Have thine own way, Lord, have thine own way,

Thou art the potter, we are the clay.

Mold us and make us after thy will,

While we are waiting yielded and still.

Have thine own way, Lord, have thine own way,

Hold o'er our being, absolute sway,

Fill with thy Spirit 'Till all shall see

Christ only always, living in me.' As the song was concluded, Tammy sat down and Pastor Bob asked the congregation to stand for prayer. "Howard, will you please lead us?"

Howard bowed his head and began to pray, "Blessed Jesus, we come to you tonight seeking your will concerning a place in the sun for the homeless children that populate the cities of America, for you said, 'Suffer the little children to come unto me and forbid then not, for of such is the kingdom of Heaven'. We know you will provide the directions and will provide the means if we just submit ourselves to you. Give us wisdom tonight and a heart that hungers to do thy will. Amen"

"Thank you, Howard. Now as we continue this meeting I'd like Robert Warren to come and give us his dream that God has laid on his heart. Robert!"

Robert strode to the podium and stood for a few seconds with his head bowed in prayer. Then he began to speak. "I've felt a call on my life for quite some time, not for the ministry in a pulpit but to minister to children that are either in foster homes or on the street. Right now, in New York City, I've been ministering to a girl that Tina won to the Lord just before she and Tammy came out here. The foster parents have not been hostile to me but have no interest in attending church or allowing Sarah to go. Sarah can't remember her parents. She doesn't know whether they are dead or alive. She says she has never lived in any foster home longer than six months. It is children like this that the Lord has laid on my heart. He has suggested a ranch with water on it. Personally, I'd like to see a place where we could have horses and water to swim in like a small lake. Naturally, there'd have to be some sort of housing.

These are just suggestions. Let God lead you in what He wants you to do. Thank you."

As Robert sat down, Pastor Bob asked for comments from the congregation.

David stood up. " We have several acres near Lake Pleasant just above Sun City on the far side of the lake. We would be willing to donate that if you want it."

Another member of the congregation arose. "I am a builder. I'd be willing to build a big ranch house or cabins, if the church can help finance the materials."

One of the ladies stood up. Our group can make clothes for the children and some might even be willing to be house mothers.

Another man stood up, "We raise horses. We can furnish both male and female so the children could learn to raise them and learn how to care for them as well as learn to ride."

Pastor Bob stood to his feet. "I am overwhelmed," he said. "I had no idea you would all be so generous. I am confident that this is of the Lord. Do you think we could get together on Saturday while

Tammy and the Pharmacist

Robert is still here and go look at this property? Those who can go, please raise you hands."

At least twenty persons raised their hands. Would about ten AM be OK? Are there any objections?"

"The only one I would have is how far it is from the church. I believe any program we support should have good sound Christian instruction. We might even have to have a Christian school for them. And a bus to bring them to church"

"Now that's what I consider good constructive thinking." Pastor Bob said. "Looks like this project is a go!"

"Okay. All those wanting to go see the land Saturday, be here promptly at nine AM. David, you'll be here to guide us? All right. Next week we'll get together and form a committee so everything will happen in proper order. We'll say good-night to all now and God bless every one of you."

Saturday morning more than thirty people showed, counting Howard's group. With David and Valerie in the lead they started out like a caravan. It was less than an hour to the site he wished to show them. Everyone was ecstatic. It was a beautiful site. About ten acres with other vacant land adjacent to it. Everyone there wanted the church to have it for a children's ranch. All they had to do was formalize it! " David. I can't thank you enough." Said Pastor Bob. "God bless you!"

Pastor Bob and most of the others turned to go but David and Valerie and Howard and his family stayed to show Robert and Tammy the lake which was not as small as they thought it would be. " God knew all the time where he wanted his ranch to be. " Hallelujah!" Robert crowed. "Wow," I have to get back here real soon. I checked out some of the auto agencies yesterday and a couple of them were interested in me so I'll probably go back and wind up things at home and be back here next week come Thursday. I'll probably sell my car and fly back like Tammy did. I can usually get a car to drive at the agency I work for".

Naturally the girls were ecstatic and wishing they could live n such a place, too. Soon Howard and Ella and the girls headed for home, leaving Robert and Tammy to go their own way.

CHAPTER THIRTY-FIVE

As the others left, Robert turned to Tammy. "Would you like to go someplace for lunch," he asked. "It's almost noon."

"Sure, whatever you'd like to do."

"OK, let's just drive until we find a place. You were going to tell me about your job. Do you like it?"

"Oh, it's fantastic. Right up my alley. Everything I'd been trained for. I'm both an auditor and a bookkeeper. I have my own office and a great computer. I work from eight to five, five days a week with two weeks vacation. I get paid on the first and the fifteenth of the month. I have a great boss and I get two thousand dollars a month!"

"Wow!" Robert cried. "That's great! And didn't somebody say something about your mother selling her house and coming out here, too?"

"Yes. I don't know how soon that will be but it looks like we all might be transplants."

"Do you suppose we might be able to work together on this project? I never said anything before but I have a strong affection for you and I'd like to get to know you better in a personal way. Would you object to that?"

"Hmm. You mean you'd like to sort of lasso and tie me so there would be no competition?"

"Well, yes, since you put it that way. There's a lot of guys out here that might get interested in you and I want to get in on the ground floor."

"So what would you like to call it? Going steady or what?"

"Well, to put it frankly, I'd like to be engaged. I was heading in that direction when you up and left!"

"I see. But aren't there some words that are usually spoken before people become engaged?"

"Tammy, you're teasing me, aren't you? Okay, I'm in love with you and I want you to marry me. Will you?"

"Will I what?"

"Will you marry me?"

"Yes. Sorry about teasing you."

Robert stopped the car and pulled over to the side of the road. He reached for Tammy and pulled her into his arms. "This is what I've been wanting to do for a long, long time." He said as he kissed her."

"And this is what I've been wanting you to do for a long time", she said as she leaned over to be kissed again.

Finally Robert started the car and they drove until they spotted a small lunchroom. Howard pulled into a parking spot and came around to help Tammy out. Clinging to his arm, they went in.

After the waitress came and gave them a menu, Robert searched in his pocket and brought out a small box. He left it beside his plate as the waitress came back for their order." I think I'll just have a cheeseburger with lettuce, onion and tomato. What would you like, Tammy?"

"I think I'll have the same and a strawberry milkshake"

"Give me a milk shake, also, but make it chocolate."

As the waitress left, he picked up the little box and opened it. "I know I should do this on bended knee but you won't make me do that here, will you?" Then he reached over and slipped a beautiful ring on her finger.

"Oh, Robert, It's beautiful. You really *were* going to ask me, weren't you?"

"Yes, I was planning on it. Can I come around and kiss you now?"

"Can't we wait until we get back in the car?"

"No, it's supposed to be done when you get the ring."

"But all these people!"

"They'll love it. Just you wait and see."

He came around the table, tipped her face up and gave her a big kiss. All the patrons broke into applause and some came over and congratulated them.

When their order came, they hurried to eat so they could get back in the car where they could kiss in private. Then drove away.

"You know, Mom said she wanted to sell her house and buy one here for us to live in. I think she was planning for us to live together but that would hardly work now, would it?"

"She is so good with children. Maybe she would be willing to be a housemother. We'll need more than one. I think we should make cabins on that land rather than one big house, don't you? I wouldn't suggest that to her though. It would be better if she felt the call to do something like that on her own.."

"I agree with you on that. But she would make a wonderful house mother. It was her teaching that enabled Tina to know how to win Sarah to the Lord. I was amazed when I heard her counseling Sarah and telling her who Jesus was. I hope whoever is a housemother teaches the boys and girls how to win others."

"Well, I guess those are things we'll have to leave with the Lord. Do you want to go back to Howard's house now?"

"Yes, I know Ella is dying to know how our day turned out. She's been teasing me about you and I put her off because I had no idea you felt this way. I think Tina will be happy, too."

"Well, here we are. Let's go in and see what they have to say."

Ella was there to open the door. "You're back early," she said, "Did you have a good time?"

"Yes, we did "Tammy said, flashing her ring.

"Ooh, I just knew it. See, I told you so. Howard! Come here! See what Tammy has." The girls came running also.

"You two really stole a march on us, didn't you? Did you bring the ring with you, Robert?'

"Sure did! I wasn't taking any chances some guy out here might horn in on my territory before I could get back here."

"More power to you, boy." Howard replied.

The girls were stunned. Here they were planning on being sisters. Now it would all be changed. Neither of them realized it would be different once Tammy got a house. They both loved Robert, though, and were glad it was him instead of some stranger. Of course, Tammy would have to call her mother and tell her the news but knowing her Mom she knew she would take it in her stride. For now Robert will have to fly back to New York tomorrow so he can wind up his business there and get back here for the next meeting. He knew he couldn't bring Sarah because there was no place for her yet.

But the Lord knew and his plans were all working out just as He planned.

"Howard," Tammy said, "have you received your telephone bill yet?"

"No I haven't, why?"

"Well, I want to pay for all these calls. Now that I have a good job, I can afford to pay for them. I still have to call my Mom and I don't feel comfortable using the phone like that unless I can pay for them. I have the money from my car so I can use some of that until I have a payday."

"You are perfectly welcome to use it. I hope you know that. But if it makes you feel better I'll show you the bill when it comes. We can talk more then. Now you go ahead and call your mother. I'm sure she'll be as happy as we are about you and Robert even though she hasn't met him yet. Maybe she'll want to talk to him, too."

"You're so right," Tammy replied. "I'll call her right now." So saying, she picked up the phone and dialed her mother's number. "Hi, Mom," she said as her mother answered.

"Oh, Tammy, I'm so glad you called. I've got a buyer for my house! They want to close right away. Can you rent a house? I'm going to have a moving-van bring my furniture out and I'll fly out."

"Mom, you sure surprised me. I called to see if you could come out soon. There's going to be a wedding and I wanted you to be here!"

"Wedding? Who?"

"Your only daughter and Robert Warren. You've never met him but you're going to love him almost as much as I do. We can't have a wedding without the mother of the bride, now can we?"

"But how could this happen so soon?"

"We've known each other for a long time. He's the one who led Howard to the Lord and helped us get our things together and get on the plane to come out here. I didn't know he felt this way about me until he came out here for this special meeting about getting a ranch for children. He brought an engagement ring with him to make sure he sealed the bargain until he can wind things up in New York and get back here."

"Well, fancy that!"

"Yes. So how soon will your closing be? Gee, I sure wish I could be there to help you. But, knowing you, you've probably got a lot of things packed already."

"I talked with the people that will do the closing and they said it would take at least a week so you'd better allow me two weeks. If you find a house and they want a contract right away, just let me know how much and I'll send it to you. I think I'll just sell my car and get a new one when I get there."

"Oh, Mom, this sounds so wonderful. And Robert is a car salesman and he can get you a good deal when you're ready. He's going to look for one for me, too. I'm using Ella's right now. Would you like to say 'hello' to Robert?"

"Yes, I sure would!"

"Robert, Mom would like to say hello to you."

Robert took the phone, "Hello, Mom, sorry to surprise you like this. Tammy was surprised, too, as she had no idea I cared for her this way. I just was taking no chances that she might meet somebody else before I had a chance to court her a little bit."

"I like your style, young man and I'm looking forward to meeting you in person. Just one thing. NO wedding until I get there. OK?"

Robert, laughing, "Right. Tammy wouldn't hear of it anyway."

"Well, if I can manage it, I'll see you in about two weeks. Now, I'd better say 'goodbye' to Tammy and sign off."

"OK, here she is." And he handed the phone to Tammy.

"Sounds like you and Robert hit it off OK" she said.. I'll send you a letter with all the details, like Mother of the bride, etc. etc. I'll also let you know of any houses that we think you'd like and the prices. Do you want two or three bedrooms?"

"Better be three. Until we know what you and Robert will be doing."

"OK, 'Bye now. I love you." Turning to the others in the room. "Well, you know what we will have to do in the next couple of weeks. Robert will be going back to New York tomorrow and, the Lord willing, will be back the following Thursday. All of a sudden, life has become a bit complicated again. Howard, can you look up rentals on the computer? I know I'm not going to have time to look. I think they can give you all the details on the computer as to the locality, price, number of rooms, etc. Would you do that for me?"

"I sure will and print out them for you. We could probably go out in the evenings and look at some as it stays light for a long time here."

"Thank you, that's wonderful. When you print them out, will you make two copies and I can send one to Mom"

"Y'know, I've an hour or so before dinner. I think I'll do that before dinner. Would you and Robert want to come in while I do it?"

"Of course," they said as they followed him to his den.

Turning on his computer, Howard brought up the local real estate market. Then began to surf different localities and looking especially for rentals. He soon found several in Glendale. "Here we are. There are several three bedroom/2 bath homes. Here's one right near our house, just a couple of streets away. There are several in North Phoenix also. Maybe it would be a good idea if we sent a street map for both cities and mark where the rentals are located."

"I agree," Tammy replied. Just then, Ella called them for dinner.

After dinner, Robert and Tammy excused them-selves saying they were going for a drive. Robert wanted to see Sky Harbor at night and look at other sites around Phoenix.

Grinning, Howard said he thought Sky Harbor was a good place to smooch.

Ella said, "Now, Howard, you quit teasing them!"

"Okay," Howard replied, "I'll behave. Go have fun, you two."

Robert grinned, "All right. We'll be back around ten-thirty. I want to have a good night's sleep before we go to church in the morning. Then I'll have to sail away into the 'wild blue yonder'. I'll be glad when I don't have to be separated from all of you in a few weeks. 'Bye."

Tammy just waved to them and went out the door with Robert.

CHAPTER THIRTY-SIX

Robert handed Tammy into the car and then strode around to the driver's side. Getting in, he reached over and drew her closer to him, then kissed her

"Robert" she remonstrated. "They might be watching, especially the girls."

"They're just going to have to get used to it," he responded. "I don't have much time to cement our relationship."

"I'll still be here when you get back. Do you plan on being back for next Thursday?"

"Unless something happens to intervene, I'll be back for good!"

"Oh, Robert, that would be wonderful, but where will you live?"

"Don't say anything yet but Iris said she would rent me a room until we get married and get ourselves a house. How do you like then apples?"

"Well, I'm just flabbergasted! When did all this come about?"

"Last night when I was leaving to go back to the motel. She said she would rent the room for the same rate I was paying at the motel, including room and board. I couldn't turn that down, could I? Especially when I would have you right next door."

"I guess the Lord *is* behind all this. When Ella kidded me about you, I said if it was his will, I would be happy about it. Wait until she hears about this."

"Oh, she already knows! I told her this morning the first thing."

"Well, I never! And she never said a word to me."

"I know. I asked her not to. I wanted to tell you myself."

"I guess that solves one problem, doesn't it? Does that mean when you come back next Thursday, it will be for good?"

"Sure does. I have two offers from automobile agencies for salesman jobs with a draw so I will have an income. I also have quite a bit of money salted away for a contingency such as this."

"You continually amaze me! And the Lord amazes me, too. He had all this worked out. All we had to do is follow his leading. Praise his name."

"Amen! Aren't we almost to Sky Harbor now?"

"Not really. I just suggested that so we could get out of the house to talk without everybody else chiming in. Some things are private. Right?"

"I guess so. Everything is moving so fast I'm having a hard time keeping up with it."

"When I get back, do you think we could go have a talk with Pastor Bob and get a date set for the wedding?"

"We can't do anything like that until Mom gets here. She has a right to be in on something as important as this."

"I agree, but she'll be here within a couple of weeks and she knows we're going to get married. What we have to discuss with Pastor Bob doesn't concern anyone but the two of us. There'll be plenty of time for her to be in on everything else. "You want a church wedding, don't you?"

"Yes, of course."

"Then the rest will follow. We may have to rent a house until the Lord shows us what part He wants us to play in the children's ranch. It wouldn't do for us to buy one right away and we can't come in and live with Howard and Ella, so while we're looking for a house for your Mom, I think we should be looking for one for ourselves."

"I guess you're right, but Robert, don't you have any family that you'd want to invite to our wedding?"

"Both my Mom and Dad are dead and I don't have any brothers or sisters. Mom and Dad died when I was around twelve years old in an auto accident. I lived with my grand-mother until she died, then I was on my own. I guess that's why I'm interested in children like Sarah."

"Oh, Robert, I'm so sorry. I guess we'll have to let Howard and Ella be stand-ins for your parents. Unless you have friends you'd rather invite for that job."

"No, they've been like parents to me. I'd like them to have that honor."

"Well, I guess I'll have to start looking for a wedding dress. I thought I'd ask Dorothy and Tina to be junior brides maids, then Valerie to be matron of honor and Lucy a bridesmaid. Mom will be the mother of the bride. Should we ask Ella to stand-in as mother of the groom? And what about your best man? And who shall we have as ushers? There should be at least two."

"How about Tom and George?"

"Great! And who will be your best man?"

"I'd like Howard to have that honor. I think he's a great guy."

"Well, that's that! I don't know about wedding invitations. Most of the people in New York couldn't afford to fly out here and it's a long, long drive to come out for just a couple of days. Then there's the reception afterwards! We can't afford to have a big reception. Maybe we should just have a catered dinner at someone's house. Maybe the pastor will have some ideas about that. They have a big hall at the church and I think a lot of the women might pitch in and help just for the privilege of being included in the wedding."

"Now you're talking. So shall we make a date with him for when I get back?"

"Yes, I agree it's a good idea considering the situation. It would have to be in an evening or on a Saturday since I have to work five days a week. If he would prefer a Sunday afternoon, that would work alright too."

"Well, I'm glad that's settled. My mind will be more at ease when I have to fly back tomorrow."

"I sure wish you didn't have to go!"

"Well, come closer to me so I can hug you a bit before we go back to the house. I sure do love you and I can't wait until we can be together for good." He gathered her up in his arms and began to kiss her.

She kissed him back, kiss for kiss until she was breathless, then said, "I do think we'd better start back, don't you? It's after nine o'clock and it will take a little while 'till we get back to Howard and Ella's home."

"OK. We'll start back, but I don't really want to."

"I know. But we do have to be sensible, and obedient to the Lord. Could we have a word of prayer before we start back?"

"Yes," he said as they bowed their heads. " We believe you have put us together and we want to do everything right in your sight. Help us to be patient and keep us both safe until we can come together again. Thank you for all the provisions you have made for us. In the blessed and Holy name of Jesus we ask it." Then he drove off toward Howard and Ella's house. The lights were still on at the house so Howard parked in the driveway, then came around to help Tammy from the car then they went in. Howard and Ella were still up but the girls had gone to their room.

"Well, hello, you two." Howard said, "How was Sky Harbor?"

"Oh, we never got there!" Robert replied. "We were too busy making wedding plans."

"You sure aren't letting any grass grow under your feet, are you?" Howard retorted.

"Well, I wanted to go have a talk with Pastor Bob before I left and one thing led to another. Tammy thought we ought to wait until her mother gets here but I said this was just between the two of us and the Pastor so she agreed. Then we talked about who we'd like to be in the wedding and how in the world we could afford a reception, etc. Since both my parents are dead, we wondered if you would stand-in as parents for me? That would make Ella as mother of the groom. And Howard would you be my best man?"

"Now you've taken my breath away!" Howard exclaimed.

"Mine, too," Ella said.

By this time, both girls were downstairs with their robes on. "What about us?" they asked.

"How about Junior bridesmaids?" Tammy interposed.

Both girls squealed in delight. "Oh, I'm so happy, Tina cried.

"Me, too," Dorothy cried.

"Ella. You would act as mother of the groom. Also, I thought I'd ask Valerie to be my Matron of Honor. All we need is a flower girl and perhaps a ring-bearer. Know anyone that would have children that age?"

"Maybe at school, there would be children that age, or perhaps the pastor would have some children in mind." Ella remarked. "But what about the Reception"

"Well, we thought about that, and we thought we ought to talk about that with the pastor, too. "I think a lot of people would want to come to the wedding and the reception so we thought if we had one in the church basement, everyone who wanted to come would have to bring a special dish or a dessert.

We could even have a sign-up sheet telling what they will bring, like one column for main dishes, another for salads and another desserts. That way we'd know what we'd have." Tammy replied."

"Well, looks like you two really have this thing pretty well organized." Howard spoke up. "When is all this going to take place?"

"Not until Tammy's mother gets here, which is about two weeks. Then Tammy will have to get a wedding dress. She wants to wait until her Mom gets here. She thought maybe the three of you could do that, Ella."

"Oh, I'd love that!" Ella cried.

"We'll have to decide what our color scheme will be so we can coordinate the bridesmaids and flower-girls dresses. We might be able to get the flowergirl's dresses and look at brides-maids dresses. Of course, they'll have to be fitted and maybe shortened. All these things take time so we can't wait until the last minute to do them. Lilac is my favorite color so I'd like those persons to wear that if possible.

"I think there are some bridal shops that stay open in the evening. Maybe we can go some evening and see what they have." Ella offered.

"Yes, I think that's what we'll have to do."

"Well, now that you've got that all ironed out, I think I'll go back to my lonely motel room and see if I can sleep," Robert opined. "See you at church in the morning. Goodnight."

Tammy walked him go the door and stepped outside to kiss him goodnight." He wrapped his arms around her as they kissed, then turned and walked to his car.

Tammy watched him go, then walked back into the house. "If you don't mind," she said. "I think I'll go upstairs and go to bed. I'm exhausted."

"You go right ahead," Ella replied. "We're going, too, as we want to be up bright and early to go to church."

Tammy turned to go upstairs as Howard turned out the lights and locked the door, then turned and followed the others.

CHAPTER THIRTY-SEVEN

Everybody was up early Sunday morning to get ready for church. Robert, too, was there ready to take Tammy. He wanted to be there especially early so he could talk to Pastor Bob about their wedding plans. He was hoping they could talk to him right after the service as his plane was scheduled for take-off at three P.M. and he wanted this interview done before he left for New York. He had looked up the scripture, which he hoped Pastor Bob would use. Fortunately, Pastor was there early and they were able to talk to him. He assured them that he would take time after the service to counsel with them. Robert heaved a big sigh of relief as they went into the sanctuary.

"What scripture were you hoping he would use in counseling with us?" Tammy asked.

"It's the one in Ephesians where Paul likens the responsibility of both husband and wife. I'm sure you are acquainted with it."

"Oh, yes, where he says "husbands, love your wives even as Christ also loved the church and gave himself for it?"

"Yes, that's the one. I feel if a husband loves his wife like that there wouldn't be the problems that exist in the world today."

"You are becoming very philosophical, aren't you?"

"Yep. Better before than after. Right?"

"Yes. I don't think we'll have problems but we never know what life will bring. Guess we'd better be quiet. The service is ready to start. As she spoke the music started and the people began to clap in time to the music, then started to sing a song of worship. After several songs, one of the associate pastors came up and gave an invitation to all who needed healing or who needed a savior and wanted to yield to Him that morning. Robert and Tammy were astounded when Tom and Lucy came forward, then David and Valerie. Not far behind came Iris and George. Tammy and Robert went up to counsel and pray with those at the altar. What a glorious service that was. Howard and Ella were ecstatic. They noticed that Dorothy and Tina were among the altar workers, ministering to the teenagers who came up to give their lives to Jesus! What a beautiful sight!"

As the people wended their way back to their seats, the song director began to sing another song, then played their instruments softly as the offering was being taken up.

Then Pastor Bob stood to begin his sermon. "I wish to speak this morning from Ephesians, chapter five, 1-12 and 22-33 "Be ye therefore followers of God, as dear children and walk in love, as Christ also hath loved us, and hath given himself for us an offering and a sacrifice to God for a sweet-smelling savor. But fornication, and all uncleanmess, or covetousness, let it not once be named among you, as becometh saints; neither filthiness, nor foolish talking, nor jesting, which are not convenient but rather giving of thanks.For this ye know, that no whoremonger, nor unclean person, nor covetous man, who is an idolater, hath any inheritance in the kingdom of Christ and of God. Let no man deceive you with vain words: for because of these things cometh the wrath o God upon the children of disobedience. Be ye not therefore partakers with them. For you were sometimes in darkness but now are ye in the light of the Lord; walk as children of light, and have no fellowship with the unfruitful works of darkness, but rather reprove them. For it is a shame even to speak of those things which are done of them in secret." "I'm quite sure that you all are aware of what Paul is talking about now. I've been hearing quite a lot about teen-age boys looking for pornography on the computer. Probably there are girls doing that, too, but what I've been hearing about is boys like 12 to 16 and 17 years old. There is no future for anyone involved in such things. It is just one more tool Satan uses to get you in his net and you can end up in the flames of hell for all eternity. Drugs are another tool Satan is using to destroy our young people. I want to insert another scripture here in this same chapter in the 13th verse. But all things that are reproved are made manifest by the Light (Jesus Christ) for whatsoever doth make manifest is light. 15,

See that you walk circumspectly, not as fools, but as wise.

Another problem we have in the world is unfaithfulness between marriage partners. Listen to what He says to them in verse 22 of this same chapter. Wives, submit yourselves unto your own husbands, as unto the Lord. For the husband is the head of the wife, even as Christ is the head of the church, and he is the savior of the body. Therefore as the church is subject unto Christ, so let the wives be to their own husbands in everything. Husbands, love your wives, even as Christ also loved the church, and gave himself for it; that he might sanctify and cleanse it with the washing of water by the word. That he might present it to himself a glorious church, not having a spot or wrinkle, or anything such thing; but that it should be holy and without blemish; so ought men to love their wives as their own bodies. He that loveth his wife, loveth himself. For no man yet ever hated his own flesh; but nourisheth and cherisheth it, even as the Lord loves the church.

"You see, both these problems are from Satan and one is kin to the other. Problems with our children are usually caused by a lack of love in the home. Fathers who don't love their wives also have problems with discipline in the home. If you're planning on getting married, both parties should make their peace with the Lord first. Then they are ready for marriage, not before. Teen-age children who are using the computer to boost their ego are making a dreadful mistake by trying to cover their lack of parental love with what they think is love on the computer. I would urge parents to put a lock on what their children can find on the computer, or else lock it altogether. The computer can be a wonderful tool to help with homework and there are a lot of clean, fun games but parents have to exercise control. Bad grades should mean no computer games until they bring their grades up. And then there should be a limit to what they can watch! This is real love! Children may not think so but some day they will thank you for it. And ALWAYS show them lots of love. You know, most medicines don't taste good but they cure what ails you so take your medicine today which is poured out to you with all the love I know to pour into it. I know this has been a long sermon but I want to extend another invitation. If you've been having problems like this, come up here this morning and let the Master problem-solver do a makeover on you. Will you come?"

Then the musicians started to play a hymn of invitation. Husbands with their wives started up the aisle, then crowds of teen-age boys and girls began streaming up the aisle, tears running down their cheeks. Tammy and Robert, then Dorothy and Tina went up to pray for them, Howard and Ella came up and started to minister as well as others from the congregation.

Tammy and Robert knew that the pastor wouldn't have time this morning to talk about their plans but God had done it using the very scriptures they were asking for. What a wonderful service it turned out to be! Tammy and Robert had planned to have a bite to eat on the way to the airport so, once the service was ended, they slipped out a side door. Robert had put his suitcases in the car when he left the motel and had paid his bill. Tammy would take the car back later as it had been paid for a month. Tammy asked Ella to tell The Pastor that she would call him and explain later. Now she and Robert were going straight to the airport and would get something to eat there. They felt like they were being torn apart but knew it would only be a few days till he was back for good. He had her mother's phone number and address and would call her when he got home. And, of course, he would be calling Tammy every night.

At the airport, he took her to an eatery and they got some supper and sat there and talked since she couldn't go through the gate with him. Just three days and then he would be back! The last few minutes, they spent in prayer for his safe return there and back, and for her mother's trip, which she would be taking soon. What a whirlwind these few days had been. "I think I'll try to go over and talk to the pastor tomorrow night and tell him what our plans are, or would you rather I wait until you get back. When I think of it that might be better because I have to look for a house for mom."

"Yes, I think that should be your first priority. We can't do too much about the reception until we know when the wedding will be and it will have to be coordinated with the schedule the church has. I think we could talk to him when I get back next week. I think it's time for me to go now, I just heard them announce my plane."

"I'm going to miss you," she said as she hugged him. He gave her a long kiss and then turned and hurried away. She was sure she saw tears in his eyes. And her eyes were far from dry either. She watched out the window as his plane taxied out to the runway, then took off. Drying her eyes she went out to the parking lot and turned the car toward Howard and Ella's house. Locking the car she stuck the keys in her purse and went in the house. They were all waiting for her.

"Well, I see Robert got off ok.' Howard said.

"Yes," Tammy replied. "It was hard saying good-bye."

"But wasn't that some service this morning? A lot of teen-agers went up. I see Dorothy and Tina were up there ministering, too. They're going to be a great addition to the ranch when we get it."

"Yes, we were so proud of them. I can't wait 'till we get it started."

"Were Iris and George there? I didn't see them."

"Yes, they were near the back. They got in a little late. I guess next time I'll have to save a couple seats for them. Did Robert tell you she offered to rent him a room when he comes back?"

"Yes, of course. He had to make it look like he was keeping an eye on me." Laughing. "He's going to call Mom when he gets home to see if she will need any help. I don't know how he's going to do it and get back here by Thursday."

"Well, he's pretty resourceful. I think he'll do just about anything he sets his mind to." Ella said.

"By the way, Howard, did you do anything yet with that list of houses? I think I'd better go out tomorrow night and see what I can find. Would you guys care to go?"

"Oh, yes, I'd like that and I think the girls would like doing that, too. How about that, girls? Naturally Howard will go. Right, honey?"

"Yep. Nothing I'd like to do better right now."

"Do you have a City Map of Glendale? Is there one on the computer? Maybe I could plat out some possibilities tonight. Could you help me with that, Howard?"

"Sure, anybody else want to come help?"

Both girls wanted to help. Ella begged off so the others went to see what they could find on the computer."

Howard put the computer on and went to Yahoo, hoping to find what they were looking for there. Sure enough when Howard brought up Arizona and then Glendale, they found a street map where they could high light a certain area they wanted to see. First they looked for the street where they lived, then spread out to the surrounding area. Howard had found a couple of houses that were for rent not too far from where they lived."

"Can you print out a copy of that map so we can take it with us?" Tammy asked.

"Sure. It'll take just a minute. Maybe I'd better make a couple so we can all look."

"That's great! Look, here's a house just a couple of blocks away. Maybe we should call and see if we can look at it tomorrow night." Tammy said.

"There's a telephone right here on the desk. Go ahead and call if you wish."

"What is the number there?"

Howard gave her the number and she dialed it. When a man answered she said, "I'm looking for a house for my mother to rent. She's moving out here from New York and I need to have something for her to move her furniture into. Could we see it tomorrow evening? I work at Motorola and can't come in the day-time."

"Certainly. I'll be glad to show it to you tomorrow evening. Would about six-thirty be OK?"

"Yes, that would be fine for us. My name is Tammy Waring and yours is?"

"Bert Lansing"

"Thank you, Mr. Lansing. We'll see you tomorrow night."

Howard didn't find any others near-by and they didn't think they'd have time to do more than one each evening anyway so they didn't try to find anymore at that time. Tammy would like to see her mother settled near Ella and Howard anyway so she wouldn't get lonely.

It had been a long day so Tammy said she'd like to go to bed if they didn't mind.

"Not a bit," Ella said, and you girls have to get up in the morning for school so you'd better get to bed, too."

Ella and Howard locked the doors and turned off the lights and soon followed them, and the house settled down and became quiet.

CHAPTER THIRTY-EIGHT

Howard went to work, the girls went to school and Tammy went to her job. Ella did the laundry and tidied up the house and it seemed like no time at all when Howard and the girls came home for lunch. She let each one make their own sandwiches, have a glass of milk and a piece of fruit as she didn't have time to make anything cooked. She'd make up for it for dinner, she said to herself.

After dinner that evening, they hurried to go see the house Tammy had called about for her mother. It was only about three blocks from Ella's house. They hoped it would be a nice house. They were pleasantly surprised by the exterior, which was landscaped beautifully. Hoping the inside was just as nice, they went up and rang the door-bell. Bert Lansing came to the door to welcome them. He showed them through the house, which had two bedrooms and two baths in addition to a lovely white kitchen, a dining area and a screened lanai by the living room. Tammy felt it would be just the right size for her mother. She asked how much the rent was and whether a lease would be required. He said $500 a month with a first and last month's deposit. Tammy also asked whether the owner would consider selling it if her mother was interested. Mr. Lansing said he thought that could be arranged since he was the owner. Noticing that the man was a very nice looking gentleman Tammy wondered whether he was married or had lost his wife. Being quite sure her mother would love this house she asked if she could give him five hundred now and another five hundred when her mother came to move in. He was agreeable with that so Tammy wrote him a check for the five hundred dollars and she signed the agreement which he had brought with him, filling in her mother's name and putting Howard's address on the form. 'Thank you for showing us the house at night," she said. "I'm sure my mother will love it."

"How old is your mother? he asked.

"Sixty-seven." Tammy replied. "I think her furniture will arrive in another week or so. May we have a set of keys so we can let the movers in when they come?"

"Certainly, here you are." He said as he handed her the keys.

'When they got home, Tammy thought she'd better call her Mom and let her know about the house. "I know it's three hours later there but I'll need to have the deposit that I put down on the house to hold it. She can wire it to me tomorrow. "Is it all right if I call her now?"

"Why don't you let us loan it to you?" Ella asked. "She might think something terrible had happened and have a stroke or heart attack. You can call her at dinnertime tomorrow evening. That way it won't be a shock to her."

"You're right. I guess I just wasn't thinking and I'd appreciate it if you could lend me the money, as I will have to put a deposit on our wedding garments, too. I didn't know how

I was going to manage it all."

"That's okay and you don't have to repay it all at once. Just do it as you can afford it."

CHAPTER THIRTY-NINE

The next morning as they were having breakfast, Tammy said to Ella, "Now that we have all the persons picked out for the wedding, and we have a house for Mom to move into I guess we'd better go looking for a wedding dress and bridesmaid dresses. Wednesdays and Thursdays are pretty well taken up by church affairs so that means we only have Tuesdays and Fridays to shop. I have a feeling that Saturdays are going to be filled with doing things on the Children's ranch! So Ella, how about you and I and the girls going shopping tonight? Will you look up some bridal shops and see if any of them are open at night?"

"Of course. Have you asked Valerie yet? She should go with us, too. She could meet us at the shop. You still don't have a flower girl picked out, do you?"

"I'll tell you what. I'll try calling Valerie today at work and see if she's willing to be matron of honor and, if so, if she can meet us tonight. I know this is early but if there are alterations to be done we have to give them time. A flower girl could wear most any style as long as the dress matches our color scheme. I think I'd like to ask Pastor Bob if he knows of a little girl at church that would like to be in the wedding."

"That's a good idea. I'll call about the shops and let you know."

"Ok, guess I'd better leave now. I don't want to be late for work."

At work, she started up her computer and checked her in basket to see there was anything urgent to take care of right away, then looked up Valerie's number in the phone book. Finding it, she dialed the number hoping to find Valerie at home. When Valerie answered she said."

"Hello, Valerie. It's Tammy. Robert and I are getting married and I wondered if you would be my Matron of Honor in the wedding?"

"Oh, Tammy, I would be thrilled to have a part in your wedding. When is it to be?"

"We have to talk with the pastor when Robert gets back but I think it will be on a Sunday after the morning service with the Reception in the Recreation Hall of the church. Everybody who wants to attend will be asked to provide a dish, salad or dessert. We'll put up sign up sheets so we'll know how many are coming and what they will bring. Sound like a plan to you?"

"Well, I guess so!"

"Ella is calling some bridal shops to see if they will be open in the evening. We thought we'd go over tonight and see what we can find in the way of gowns. Would you be able to meet us there? I'll call you back after Ella calls."

"Yes, I can come. Just let me know when and where."

"OK. I'll do that. I'd better get to work now. 'Bye."

About an hour later, Ella called to say she'd found a shop that would stay open that evening so Tammy called Valerie back to inform her of the name and location of the shop. They planned on being at the shop no later than 7:00 P.M.

Promptly at five o'clock. Tammy closed up her office and headed for Ella's house. Ella had dinner ready and the girls were all agog at the idea of shopping for dresses for themselves as well as Tammy's wedding dress and Valerie's gown.

"Ella," Tammy said. "I forgot to call Mom and let her know we got the house for her. Do you mind if I call her now?"

"Certainly. It's not too far to the Bridal shop. Go ahead."

Tammy dialed her mother's number and was happy to find her at home. "Mom, she said, "We got you a house last night but it would have been too late to call you when we got home. It's a beautiful house with beautiful landscaping for only five hundred dollars a month with first and last months rent in advance. He let me just put five hundred down to hold it . You can pay the other five hundred when you move in. Sound OK?

"Yes, that's wonderful. I'll wire you one thousand tomorrow, so you won't be broke."

"Thank you, Mom. I appreciate that. I have to go now as we're going to a bridal shop right after dinner to get the wedding gowns. Tina and Dorothy are going to be Junior bridesmaids. We'll take you shopping when you get here. "Bye, now."

Howard, too, would need to rent a tuxedo, although probably not at this store so he decided to stay home and let the women have their evening to themselves. He said they should go ahead and he'd rid up the table and load the dishwasher.

"When they arrived at the store, Valerie was already there. They decided to look for full-length dresses for the two girls first. Tammy had decided to use contrasting colors that would compliment them, one in a rosy pink and the other in lilac. Since Dorothy was blond, they decided to use lilac for her. Tina, who had dark hair would wear the pink. The clerk went to see what she could find in those colors and came back with an armload. Most of them were strapless but Tammy thought they could wear them later with little lacy bolero jackets.

The clerk said, "We have some if you'd like to see them."

"Oh, yes, if you would please. "

Valerie spoke up, "If you have something like the lilac for the maid of honor, I'd like to see that, please."

"Certainly, I'll be right back."

In just a few minutes, she came back with a beautiful dress in lilac satin and several boleros for the girls to try on.

Needless to say, the girls were in seventh heaven as they tried on the dresses with the little boleros over them. They liked them so well that Tammy decided not to try anymore but to concentrate on Valerie's and her own dresses.

"Are you satisfied with your dress or would you like to try some others?" the clerk asked Valerie.

"Yes, I would like to try this one on. Do you have any others styles in this same color?"

"Yes, I have a few. I'll bring some out while you try this one on for size."

"Thank you."

When the clerk came back Valerie had the dress on but it was a little too loose on her. The clerk had two more in the same color but in a different style. Valerie tried the next one on and it was just right and she just loved it. "This is fine," she said. "I'll take it."

'If you'll give me a minute I'll take these others in the back room and bring some wedding gowns out. I presume you want white?"

"Yes" Tammy replied. "Robert has never been married before and I'm wearing white for his sake. My first husband died in a terrible train accident a little over a year ago."

"Oh, how dreadful! I pray God will bless this marriage with a long, long life!"

Gathering up an armful of the dresses that were not needed, she hurried from the room and soon came back with three gowns that she thought would be appropriate for Tammy.

Tammy selected one to try on and was immediately entranced with it. Seed pearls and lace decorated the bodice and sparkles were sprinkled all over the skirt, which draped gracefully to the floor. "I don't believe I need to try the others," she said. "This one is just fine. By the way, do you have dresses for the flower girl, too?"

"Yes, we do."

"We don't have a flower girl yet but we'll bring her in as soon as we find one. Also, can we put these in lay-a-way until the week before the wedding? I just started a new job at Motorola so I won't get paid until then. I can make a deposit now. My fiancé won't be back from New York until Thursday of this week. We thought we might have to have alterations but I'm happy that won't be necessary. Would $500 be enough to hold them 'till then?"

"Yes that will be fine."

"If you will box my dress up, I'll take it with me. I'll pay for it now, of course," Valerie said.

"If you will total the rest of the garments, I'll pay you the deposit and we'll be on our way. I thank you for staying open for us." Tammy said.

"Would you believe it's only nine o'clock?" she said to Ella. I can't believe we accomplished so much in only two hours.

"Now we only need to find a flower girl and order the flowers. The guys will have to get their own tuxedos."

The clerk came with the bill and a receipt for the deposit and they were ready to be on their way home.

"Good night, Valerie. We'll see you later. Thanks again for being my maid of honor. Thank you Miss, for your help. Goodnight."

"Ella, would it be all right with you if we look for your dress another evening? I thought you might find something at a different dress shop rather than a wedding shop."

"Of course. I'm amazed that we got this much done tonight. I'm tired just watching you and the girls try things on. Let's go home. OK?"

"I say Amen to that. Let's go."

CHAPTER FORTY

Meanwhile, Robert had wrapped things up in New York. He would have liked to go up and help Tammy's Mom get her house emptied and on it's way but, since her closing was almost two weeks away, his hands were tied. He called her and offered to fly back and help her after the closing but she wouldn't hear of it. She knew Tammy needed him there. Robert wanted to get back to Phoenix so they, too, could look for a house to go to when the wedding was over. A honeymoon was out of the question until Tammy had been on the job for at least six months. And there was the matter of the children's ranch that they wanted to get going.

Robert felt an urgency about getting back there for the next meeting on Thursday night. When Tammy's Mom refused his help he made reservations to drive back there early Tuesday morning and notified Iris to let her know he'd be back then. Since he only had a furnished apartment, he had no problems with furniture but wanted to take along his computer and other equipment that he didn't want to take on a plane. And he figured he might as well keep his car rather than sell it.

He figured he'd be money ahead that way, as he wouldn't have to buy a computer or a car. I guess I'd better call Tammy tonight and let her know I'll be leaving here tomorrow morning.

Promptly at nine P.M. he dialed Howard's number and asked for Tammy. Howard answered the phone, "I'm sorry Robert but all the females in this household have gone shopping for wedding garments. Can you call back around twelve-thirty your time? I know she'll want to talk to you."

"Yes, Howard, I'll do that! Since I plan on leaving here tomorrow morning, I think I'll set the alarm clock for that time and then shower and take a nap'

"OK I'll let her know you called and that you will be calling back at nine-thirty our time. G'night"

Promptly when the alarm sounded, Robert awakened and dialed the phone.

"Hi, Tammy," he said when she came to the phone. "I'm calling to let you know I'll be leaving early tomorrow morning. I'm going to drive out so I can bring my computer and other private items that I don't want to take on a plane. I should be there in time for the meeting. Thursday night."

"Oh, Robert! That's wonderful! Please be careful. Don't take any chances. The last thing we'd want is for you to end up in a hospital somewhere! "

" Don't worry. The Lord Jesus will be my companion and He won't let anything happen to me. This is all part of his plan and he'll see me through!"

"I'll be praying until you get here. Did I tell you we found a house for Mom? It's only a couple of blocks from this house. A real nice man owns it. He wanted to know how old Mom is. I think he's about the same age and seemed to be single. Wouldn't it be something if we'd have another romance on our hands?"

"Tammy, you are just a plain romantic! You just wait until I get back there and you'll have all the romance you want!"

"Huh! Promises. Promises. I'll believe it when I see it." She giggled.

"You just remember that when you want more kisses!" he replied."

"Well, much as I hate to say it, we're going to have to hang up. We're paying for these phone calls, you know."

"What do you mean *we're* paying for them?"

"Well, when we're man and wife you'll be responsible for the bills, won't you?"

"Oh, oh, I won't touch that with a ten foot pole! I think we might have to put that in the marriage agreement when we talk to Pastor Bob."

"Honey, you know I was just teasing you. I believe as long as the wife is working, they should share the expenses according to their wages, but we'll let Pastor Bob settle that for us. "

"Good-night, darling. I was just teasing you, too. I can't wait until I can hold you in my arms again. I love you. 'Bye."

Tammy hung up and turned to Ella and Howard.

"Robert is leaving tomorrow morning to drive through. He doesn't want to bring his computer and other items by plane or have to sell them and buy others when he gets here so he feels he'd be better off financially to drive himself. I agree with him but I told him to be very careful because we didn't want to hear that he was in the hospital somewhere.

"I don't think we need to worry about that," Howard replied. "He has Jesus with him and this is part of His plan. He won't let anything interfere."

"I know that. I just can't help being a little fearful."

"You know planes do have accidents, too, "Ella said. "We just have to trust the Lord no matter where we go, even on the city streets."

"That's true. Well, I guess I'd better go up and shower and go to bed and pray for Robert to be safe and keep us all true to Him."

"Good idea," Howard and Ella replied "Good night "

CHAPTER FORTY-ONE

Wednesday night they stayed home and had family worship as they had begun when Howard first came home. He continued on in the book of John where they had left off last time. "Let's see, we were talking about baptism, weren't we?

Yes, here it is. John is telling how Jesus came to be baptized of John the Baptist. (If you are confused by two men named John, the writer of this book is Jesus' brother. The other is John the Baptist who is Jesus' cousin). Starting at John 1:23 He (John the Baptist) said, I AM THE VOICE OF ONE CRYING IN THE WILDERNESS, MAKE STRAIGHT THE WAY OF THE LORD, as said the prophet Esa'ias. And they which were sent were of the Pharisees. asked him and said unto him. Why baptizeth thou then if thou be not that Christ, nor Elias neither that prophet? John answered them saying, I baptize with water; but there standeth among you, one whom ye know not; He it is, who coming after me is preferred before me ,whose shoes I am not worthy to unloose. These things were done in Bethabata beyond Jordan, where John was baptizing.

29. The next day John seeth Jesus coming unto him, and saith, Behold the Lamb of God, which taketh away the sin of the world. This is he of whom I said, After me cometh a man which is preferred before me, for he was before me. And I knew him not but he that sent me to baptize with water, the same said unto me, Upon whom thou shalt see the Spirit descending, and remaining on him, the same is he which baptizeth with the Holy Ghost, and I saw, and bare record that this is the Son of God! Now let us go back to Matthew 3:16 &17 And Jesus, when he was baptized, went up straightway out of

the water: and, lo, the heavens were opened unto him, and he saw the Spirit of God descending like a dove and lighting on him. And lo, a voice from heaven, saying, This is my beloved Son in whom I am well pleased."

"Oh, that is so beautiful!" Ella cried. "How I wish we could get the whole world to listen to such a message as this."

"Yes, it is beautiful and this is why we are called to witness to our neighbors, our friends, our relatives and any one else who'll listen and use any means to gain their attention for it is the most precious gift anyone could offer us, the gift of salvation." Howard replied. "Tammy, I thank you again for introducing me to Him."

"It was my pleasure and my goal in life to introduce Him to everyone I possibly can," she answered.

"Shall we go to Him now in prayer?" Howard said.

"May I start?" Dorothy asked.

"Certainly," he responded.

Dorothy then began to lift her voice to this precious one of whom they had been discussing. "Dear Blessed Lord, how we thank thee for thy precious word. Thank you for being that Word ever since the beginning of time. Thank you for letting me know you now before all the worldly things could creep in.

Help me to witness to my schoolmates that they, too, might escape all the horrible things that happen when Sin comes into their life. Make me a blessing wherever I go. Amen."

Tina began to pray next. Dear Jesus. Thank you for a Godly mother and grandmother who taught me about you since I was a little child. Please continue to be with Sarah, Make it possible for her to be with us soon and remember our plans to see a ranch built here that will provide a home for many children who have no home. Bring Robert back safely. We've come to love him, too. Also, keep those who have come to know you through so simple a thing as a sing-a-long. Show us more ways to serve you. In your precious name we ask it".

Next Tammy lifted her voice in prayer. "I thank you, Lord, for these precious girls and Ella who have come to know you through the power of Howard's prayers. How precious each one is. Bless Howard as he endeavors, not only to lead his family but to witness to every one he meets whether it be friend or foe. Keep us in the hollow of thy hand. Amen.

Ella: "Howard would you pray for both of us? So many wonderful things have been brought before the Lord that I can't think of a thing to add to it."

Putting his arm around her, Howard drew her close to him, Truly we are most blessed and I say 'amen' to every prayer that has been offered. I too, am at a loss for words except to say thank you to the Lord for giving us such a wonderful family and friends. And I consider Tammy and Tina family. I also give thanks for the host of friends we have come to know since we found the Lord. Thank you, blessed Jesus. Amen." As they got up from their knees, most of them were wiping tears from their eyes.

CHAPTER FORTY-TWO

When Tammy awakened next morning she looked out her bedroom window and there, Lo and behold, she saw Robert's car parked outside Iris' house. Pulling on a robe, she went screaming down the stairs. "Robert's back! His car is parked by Iris' house. That brought the house down as every-one, Howard, Ella and the girls came tumbling down.

Robert, hearing them, came out of the house, a big grin on his face. Tammy ran to clasp him in her arms. "Oh, I'm so glad you're back. When did you get in?"

"About an hour ago. Iris was expecting me and we had to talk a bit until I knew you'd be up."

"Can you come in the house? Did you have breakfast? Ella asked.

"Yes to both questions. I know Tammy and Howard have to go to work and the girls to school. You'd better go get dressed. I'll sit here and talk to Ella while she gets your breakfast. Do you have anything new to tell me, Ella?"

"Not anything I dare talk about except Tammy's mom's house. We went and looked at it Monday night. It's only about two blocks from here so we can go back and forth and she won't need to be lonesome."

"That's nice. But what is it you can't talk about?"

"We went and got the wedding dresses Tuesday night and that's ALL I can tell you."

"I guess that's part of the excitement of a wedding, isn't it?

"Yep. You and Howard and David will have to rent tuxedos. Probably the last week before the wedding. Did we talk about having the reception at church? I know we haven't talked with the pastor yet but I couldn't remember if we'd talked about it."

"Yes, we did but couldn't plan on it until we talked to the pastor. I'm certain he'll be all for it. It sure will solve a big problem for us. I hope we hear from your Mom pretty soon that the moving van has come and she's on her way. We can't set a date until we know when she'll be here."

"Well, I know she's just as anxious as we are. I'm sure it will be soon. Anyway, we have to find us a house, too. I think we should start Saturday if we don't have to go to the ranch that day. "

"Right," Robert said. "That's something else that I think we should bring up tonight because there has to be a legal transfer of the property to the church with the stipulation that it be used for homes for homeless children. I think, too. That we should stipulate what kind of housing we want put up. Like no more than six children to a home. And teen age boys should have a separate home from the one for teen-age girls, don't you think so? Also, it would be nice to have a husband-wife team as house parents and they need to be paid so they 'll be responsible people."

"Right" Tammy responded.

Might be a good idea to have a few milk cows, too

Do you think we can make gardens here? Food will be an expensive item and we'll need to raise everything we can. We'll need a freezer, too. I think we'll have to start hitting up the merchants for donations of items like that."

"Yes, and there should be a corral for the horses. Maybe a barn. Whew! We'll sure have a lot to discuss tonight!"Robert added.

CHAPTER FORTY-THREE

The church was full for a Thursday night! Robert, Howard, David and Tammy were among those seated on the rostrum. As before Pastor Bob asked Tammy to lead a song to get the meeting started. She stood and walked to the pulpit and began to sing 'Have Thine Own Way'. The audience joined in. Robert was then asked to lead them in prayer.

"Dear Jesus" he prayed," Thank you for this opportunity to work for you. I know you are well aware of the gifts that have been offered so far. I know also that you have already blessed each giver. We pray you'll teach us how to use these gifts wisely and that many children and young people will come to know you as their Lord and Savior, Lead us tonight as we endeavor to put your plan into action. Let there be no disharmony among us. In your precious name, we ask it. Amen."

Pastor Bob stood up. Our Board of Trustees is present tonight and the Chairman of the Board, Don Thompson, would like to say a few words. Don…"

Don stood up and strode up to the rostrum. "I can just hear some of you say, oh-oh-'here comes trouble!' But I want to reassure you, we are back of you one hundred percent \We do however have certain responsibilities. We need to make sure the deed to the property is ceded to the church with the stipulation that it is to be used for a children's ranch. We need to set a criteria for those who are asking to be admitted. We also need to stipulate what kind of buildings will be erected

Since we will be paying the bills, we need to know where the money will come from to meet those bills. If any of you have questions concerning any of these statements, we will be happy to confer with you on them, either here now or at any of our board meetings. We want to work with you, not be a hindrance. Thank you."

Robert stood up. This is right along the line that we've been thinking on. I think someone should be designated as chairman of a committee to gather these pertinent facts and that committee should meet with the Board and iron out any differences of opinion. That committee should be appointed as soon as possible as we have had some wonderful offers of help besides the land David Williams has offered to give us. We need to take advantage of those offers while they are still available.'

Pastor Bob stood up. "I move that Robert Warren be named to head that committee and that he be permitted to add to his committee those whom he believes he can work with. I know, he's new here but who are we to argue with God? This is *HIS* plan. Let's bring it to fulfillment."

There were Amens all over the room."

Pastor Bob again stood up. Let's make it official. All those in favor of Robert Green as chairman of the Children's Ranch Committee, please stand up., Will the tellers please count these. (Please remain standing until you have been counted. A paper will be passed among you. Please sign your name. (If you didn't stand up but want to be counted just sign your name.)." A copy of the record of tonight's meeting will be sent to each one who signs that paper tonight".

It took a long time to get all the signatures on that paper. Many had a second thought and signed on, too. This meant that, not only would they have their backing but financial support, also. Pastor Bob was jubilant! Robert, too, was happy to be of service in this way. He expected to hear a lot of ideas and offers of service. Since the hour was getting late, he suggested they adjourn for tonight and meet again the next Thursday night.. He said he would have an agenda ready to propose then. "Pastor? Do you have anything else you wish to say?" If not, will you close our meeting with prayer?"

Pastor Don stood to his feet. "Let us all rise. Father, we bow our heads and our hearts to thee. Thank you for guiding us as we feel our way to bring into being the plan you have shown us. Thank you for the harmony we have felt here tonight. We pray there will be a generous out pouring of financial help to begin this project to fruition in a timely fashion. In the name of Jesus who said "Let the little children come unto me for of such is the Kingdom of Heaven. Amen."

The crowd milled about as they moved out, talking animatedly about the events that had happened tonight.

Robert and Tammy waited to talk with Pastor Bob about their wedding plans. It was not too long before he was free and came to talk with them. I have an idea that you're wanting to talk wedding plans," he said.

"Yes, we do. Is it too late to talk tonight? We could come over tomorrow night if that would be better." said Tammy.

"Yes, I think tomorrow night would be better. I'll need to have a church calendar so we'll know what is already on the menu."

"I think what we really wanted to do tonight is nail down when we could talk to you. You're such a busy man." Tammy said.

"Would seven-thirty be alright for you?"

"Yes, that would be fine. I work until five."

"We'll see you then. Good-night."

CHAPTER FORTY-FOUR

When they got home, Ella said she had had a call from Tammy's mother and that she would call back around ten PM.

"I wonder if anything is the matter," she said. "Mom doesn't ordinarily stay up that late." Just then the phone rang and Ella motioned for Tammy to take it.

"Hi, Tammy, I just took a chance that you would be home by now. I wanted to let you know we had the closing on my house today and the moving van will be here tomorrow morning. They said it would take about three days to drive out there so, if they leave as soon as they're loaded they should be there sometime Monday. I thought since you have to work maybe Robert would oversee putting things in place. I have tickets for American Airlines for Sunday at 7:30 AM and will arrive there around 3: PM As soon as the van is loaded I'll take the bus down to New York and get a motel to stay at until it's time for my plane. Is there a motel near the airport?"

"Yes, Mom, this is fantastic! There is a Holiday Inn at La Guardia Airport I think you can get a taxi to take you to that motel so you won't have to do anything but leave your room and go right into the airport. Oh, I'm so excited for you!"

"You did say you'd gotten a house for me, didn't you?"

"Yes, but we got a two bedroom, two bath instead of three bedrooms since Robert and I will be married by then and you won't need three bedrooms. Is that OK?"

"Yes, since I won't be buying right away. That will be ample. So when is the wedding?"

"We have an appointment with the pastor tomorrow night. Everything has sort of been on hold until we knew you'd be here. You won't have to worry about a reception or anything like that because we're going to ask the pastor to let us have it in the banquet room at the church. I do have my bridesmaids chosen. Tina and Dorothy are going to be junior bridesmaids and they are thrilled to pieces. We got their dresses the other night, and my maid of honor and my wedding dress. We put them in lay-a-way. My maid of honor paid for her dress and took it home with her. We have to get a flower girl yet and the men need to get their tuxedos. And I forgot to get a veil so you'll have to help me do that. And you and Ella will have to get your dresses. Ella is going to act as Mother of the Groom as Robert's parents are both dead. Howard will be Robert's Best Man. Wow, did I leave anything out?"

"Did you get yourself a house yet?"

"No. We'll probably do that Saturday. Working full time doesn't leave me much time and we have these meetings every Thursday night. Then tonight they made Robert the head of the committee for the children's ranch so he's going to be busy with that. I've lived a busy life since I came out here. We won't even be able to take a honeymoon because I won't get a vacation until after I've been there for six months. We're being married on a Sunday so there won't even be time for a honeymoon then. But with a new (to us) house, we'll just wait until we have a vacation. Well, guess that really is all I have to tell you. I think we'd both better get to bed, don't you?"

"Yes, I am tired but I couldn't wait to let you know

I was practically on my way."

"Oh, Mom, I'm so happy that you're finally coming.

Wait until I tell Tina in the morning. She'll be ecstatic! , Call me at your motel. I love you so much! See you Sunday. Bye."

Turning to Ella, she said. "I'm going to call Robert on his cell-phone and let him know Mom is on her way."

"You go ahead. I think I'll go to bed. Good-night."

"Good-night." Then she dialed Robert. "Robert, it's me. Mom just called. The moving van is coming tomorrow morning to load her furniture and she will take a bus to New York to a hotel at LaGuardia

Airport. Then fly out early Sunday morning and be at Sky Harbor at three P.M. on Sunday. "

"Wow! That's great. Looks like everything is coming together all at once. Praise the Lord."

"She expects the van to arrive Monday morning and she wanted to know if you would be there to help her with the furniture since I will have to be at work."

"Of course I will. Where will she sleep Sunday night?"

"She can sleep with me. I have a double bed. I'll call Mr. Lansing from work tomorrow and make sure the electricity and water will be turned on. Good-night. I love you."

"And I love YOU! See you in the morning. And don't forget! We have that appointment with the pastor tomorrow night at 7:30 P.M.'

"I'll remember and be ready."

CHAPTER FORTY-FIVE

Next morning Tammy told the girls about the phone call from her mother. Tina was ecstatic and Dorothy a little bit sorrowful because she felt that the close relationship she'd had with Tina was about to end. She couldn't see ahead to the times they would have in the future. Robert was over before they'd even had time to eat breakfast. He grabbed Tammy and whirled her around before he kissed her. "I'm so happy that the end of all this waiting is in sight! Tonight we have a session with the pastor to set the date for the wedding and finalize the ideas for the reception. Then Saturday we go house hunting for ourselves! "

"I guess I'd better finish my breakfast and be off to work."

"OK. See you tonight. Love you. 'Bye. Iris won't be very happy if she has something hot and I let it get cold." He blew a kiss to all and sailed out the door.

That evening, Robert came over for dinner as he and Tammy had that all-important meeting with the pastor to set up the final details for the wedding. As soon as dinner was over they hastened to get in the car and go to the church. They found Pastor Bob already waiting for them. "Let us have a word of prayer before we start this session because we want God's will in everything. Let us bow our heads. Father,

We come before you this evening seeking your will in all that we do. Guide us, we pray. In the name of Jesus, we ask it."

"Now, I imagine you'd like to set a date."

"Yes, but there are certain criteria we want to discuss with you first that will affect the date and possibly the time." Tammy replied.

"And what criteria is that?"

"Well, neither of us have the money to put on a big reception and we think there are a lot of people who'd like to attend it. What we want to do is have a reception in the banquet hall and have a sign-up sheet asking anyone who wants to attend the wedding to bring a dish of food – main dish, salad or dessert. That way as many as wanted to could come and we could enjoy the reception together. We feel that hurdle has to be settled first as there may be other things already on the agenda that would conflict on that particular day, if that is approved by yourself or the board. I'm sure the women's groups would be all for it."

Robert spoke up. "I think we should choose the third Sunday.

That will give us time to iron out these other difficulties. Your Mom might have some ideas, too. We may just have to have a wedding dinner for the participants in the wedding.

"While we are talking, we wondered if you knew a little girl to be the flower girl? Someone about four to six years old."

"Yes, there is a very smart little girl that would fit the bill. She's the daughter of one of the Board Members."

"Will you speak to her parents and have them get in touch with me.? Tammy asked. We'll need to get her dress if they're willing for her to be in it. We still have to get dresses for the Mother of the Bride and Mother of the Groom. Ella Peters s going to stand in for that position as Robert's parents are both dead. We also have to order flowers yet. I guess we really need that extra week.

Do you have any instructions for us other than that beautiful sermon you preached last Sunday? Also, the girls, Dorothy and Tina have been after us to find out when there will be a baptism?" Robert remarked."

There will be a baptism the Sunday following your wedding. There will be a sign-up sheet in the vestibule this coming Sunday. To get back to the wedding, I will talk to the board tomorrow at their regular meeting about the possibility of using the banquet room in the manner you suggested. I think, like you, that a lot of people would want to attend and would do as you have suggested. I'll also speak to Don Lawson whose daughter I suggested as flower girl and

Tammy and the Pharmacist

give him your name and phone number so he or his wife can make arrangements."

"Oh, thank you. I think the Lord will work all this out in a manner that will be to His glory. Tammy answered.

"Is there any other questions you need answers to? I'm confident that you and Robert have all the questions pretty well in hand."

"Probably the order of service would be the only other detail. I would prefer to leave the scriptures up to you. I can give you a list of the participants. Also Robert and I will be singing to each other so we'll need to practice with the organist or whoever will be playing We'll be singing, 'Because.' I presume you are familiar with that song? "

"Yes, I am. It is a very beautiful song."

"Thank you. Will we need to have another meeting with you and when would you prefer to have the wedding rehearsal?"

"Either Friday evening or Saturday is available. Whichever you prefer is OK with me.

"I think Saturday evening would be the best time,-for me anyway. |Also, is right after the morning service OK for the wedding ceremony?

"Yes, that will be fine –especially if the board agrees to allow the banquet room to be used as you proposed. "\

Then I guess that winds up everything for tonight. We'll wait to see what the board says before we plan any further about the reception."

"Fine. I have an idea the board will be favorable. I just find it necessary to consult them first. See you Thursday night then. OK? Pastor Bob concluded.

Both Tammy and Robert nodded and shook his hand as they prepared to leave. "Good-night."

As they went back to their respective dwelling places, Robert said, "I think we covered a lot of territory tonight, I'm satisfied, how about you?"

"Yes, I am, too. We can't always have our way but I think every is going to work out all right."

"So! How about a kiss to seal the bargain?

"Oh? You think I'm a bargain, huh?"

"Uh-huh! You couldn't very well have that nice big wedding without me. Besides, you didn't ask me whether I'd sing with you at the wedding! How do you know I don't croak like a frog?"

"I've been listening. You have a beautiful tenor voice."

"Such ego! But, yes, there wouldn't be a wedding at all without you. But I sure do love you – ego and all!

Bringing the car to a stop, Robert leaned over to collect a few kisses. "Mmm, I love you, too."

"We'd better go home now. I have to get my beauty sleep so I don't look haggard at my own wedding!"

"Nothing could make you look haggard. You're so beautiful."

"Anyway, I'm sleepy now. Can we go home now?

"O.K. he put the car into gear and drove toward home.

There were lights on in the living room at Howard and Ella's.

Robert parked the car and helped Tammy out, then clasped her in a big hug, kissing her hungrily. Then he led her to the porch opened the door for her and handed her in. "Goodnight Sweetheart, he whispered and closed the door then turned and made his way to Iris.' Both she and George had gone to bed so he went up to his room, undressed and read a scripture from his Bible, then bowed beside his bed and prayed before settling in for the night.

CHAPTER FORTY-SIX

That evening, Robert came over for dinner and they all decided to take a night off and stay at home so they could have family worship. When dinner was over and the table cleared and the dishes put in the dishwasher, they got their Bibles and gathered around the table to read His word. Howard opened his Bible to the book of John. Can one of you tell me where we were reading last time?"

"Wasn't that the chapter in Matthew, where John, the Baptist was baptizing people and Jesus came to him to be baptized? I think it was chapter three starting in the thirteenth verse" Dorothy said. Then cometh Jesus from Galilee to Jordan unto John, to be baptized of him. But John forbade him saying, I have need to be baptized of thee, and comest thou to *me?* And Jesus answering said unto him, Suffer it to be so now: for thus it becometh us to fulfill all righteousness. Then he suffered hm. And Jesus, when he was baptized, went up straightway out of the water; and, lo, the heavens were opened unto him, and he (John) saw the Spirit of God descending like a dove, and lighting on him And, lo, a voice from heaven saying, This is my beloved Son, in whom I am well pleased."

"That was beautifully done, Dorothy. You're going to make a wonderful Sunday School Teacher one of these days. Would anyone else like to comment of this portion of scripture?" Howard commented. "Robert, how about you?"

"Well, it's been my experience that when Jesus does or says something that he is setting an example for each of us to follow. In other words, when this truth is revealed to us he expects us to follow and do likewise. Have any of you been baptized yet?

Tammy and the Pharmacist

"No opportunity has been offered yet. I believe the church has a baptistery and that a baptismal service is offered every so often. We asked the pastor when the next baptismal service will be. "Howard replied. He said it will be the Sunday following our wedding. He said there will be a sign-up sheet this Sunday morning. I'm certain there are several candidates who are ready to follow the lord in baptism. There are at least four in my own household. "Are there any more comments or requests for prayer?"

"I'd like prayer that I might know God's mind on this project we're trying to build as a ranch for street children." Robert responded.

"Then let us pray," Howard replied. So saying, they all knelt.

"Dear Jesus, we're so very sure all that has happened in our lives is a part of your plan, but we want to be sure that we are doing everything just the way you want it done. "Tammy prayed. "Please give Robert the assurance and direction that he needs to accomplish these things. Make the rest of the congregation to put their shoulders to the wheel and lay it on the hearts of the business people in this community to respond to pleas for donations such as refrigerators, freezers and other appliances that will be needed so badly for this project to be accomplished successfully. And show Robert who would be the best person to head such a committee. Thank you for hearing us pray."

"Dear Jesus," Dorothy prayed. "We are all anxious to follow you in baptism. We are so happy to hear that a time has been scheduled for it. Thank you. Amen.

Howard concluded the prayer session, "We lift our voices in agreement with the petitions that have already been offered. Thank you for hearing us pray. We love you so very much. Amen. They all rose to their feet and the girls headed for their room.

Tammy slowly.walked with Robert back to Iris' house

Then he had to walk her back again and kiss her goodnight. Then she, too, had to head for bed as tomorrow would be another work-day.

CHAPTER FORTY-SEVEN

Thursday night was upon them almost before they knew it. They hurried through dinner and went on their way to the church. Robert had printed out a sheet for each possible committee to be formed. He wanted to get those committees in motion right away. He'd also made a tentative list of equipment they might need. He also wanted to talk to the man who had offered some horses to see what they would need for them. He knew they would at the very least have to have fencing. And, perhaps, a corral. He also wanted to know how many were interested in becoming house-parents. He had a big notebook and Tammy would take notes for him. Soon the building began to fill up. There were more people than had been at the first two meetings. Promptly at 7:30 he called the meeting to order and asked Howard to lead them in prayer.

Howard stepped to the mike and began to pray. "Dear Heavenly Father, we sincerely believe this project is in your divine order. We pray you will instruct us that everything will be done according to your will. In the name of Jesus. Amen.

Robert again stepped up to the mike. Tammy will be taking notes and everything that is said or done here tonight will be made a matter of record. If you are interested in heading up a certain committee, please don't hesitate to say so. Also, if we overlook a committee that needs to be formed, please feel free to say so. The more involved we become the faster this project will come together. I'm throwing the meeting open to you. Who'll be first?

Ella stood up. I would like to work with those who'd like to become house parents. We'd like to see husbands and wives involved in this phase of the project. Even children who are street children need both parents. This will be a vital part of the project

"Wonderful. Next.

David and Valerie. "We, too, would like to be involved in that phase of the work."

"Great. Please meet with Ella Peters. Any others who are interested in that phase of the project; please contact her." So that we don't get bogged down in one phase of the work. I believe I'll have Tammy read off the list of committees that are needed. Then you can let us know which one you are willing to head or would like to work on. Tammy, can you give us the list?"

First of all, we need to find donors for building materials. Which will include such things as cupboards, sinks, toilets, bathtubs or shower stalls. Electrical equipment, etc.such as airconditioning units. Someone who has expertise along these lines to head up the committee.

If the person who offered some breeding horses is here, would you please stand up? Thank you. Your name, please?

John Roberts. Would you head up a committee to direct us how we go about getting the proper equipment and to instruct the ones who will be doing the work? He nodded his head. Great!

We will also need a committee that will approach businesses that handle refrigerators, dishwashers and ranges to

See if we can get those items donated. I guess that's enough for tonight.

Each one who agrees to head a committee should endeavor to find members to be on that committee. There's plenty of work for everybody.

David, I know you agreed to donate the land but would you also see about ceding that to the church with the stipulation that it be used for a children's ranch. We won't even be able to store any equipment on it until that is done. You might need to attend a board meeting and may need an attorney. I know you're interested in being a house –parent and you can still do that but will you please head up the committee for this part of the project?"

"Certainly. I'll get on it tomorrow."

"Praise the Lord! Are there any more questions or suggestions?" 'Since there are no more, shall we adjourn until next week? All in favor, say Amen."

"A-men!

CHAPTER FORTY-EIGHT

Saturday morning Robert was over bright and early so they could go house-hunting. He and Tammy climbed in his car and they drove off. He asked."Do you have any idea where you want to look first?"

"Not really. I have this one a few blocks away. All I want to do is be sure we are in the same school district so Tina and Dorothy can still go to school together. Let's see (looking at the map) there was one a couple of streets over, if it's still available. There it is with the sign in the front yard. Can you see the phone number? Maybe we can go in and look at it"

Robert got out his cell phone and dialed the number. There was no answer, however. "Well, that must not be the right one." He said. "Let's try that house down the street. I think it has a sign in the front yard.. Yes, it is. It says FOR SALE by OWNER. Can you read me that phone number?

I'll call and see if we can look at it."

"But Robert, we can't afford to *buy* a house right now."

"I'll call anyway. You never know how things will turn out." He dialed the number and a gentleman answered.

Yes, we'd love to show it to you. We'll be right over. Take us about fifteen minutes."

They got out of the car and wandered around the grounds while they waited. "Oh, Robert, it's so beautifully landscaped. And it looks really large. There must be at least three bedrooms." How could we ever afford something like this?"

"Here they come! Let's just wait and see."

The owners drove up in a late model sedan and got out to welcome them. "By the way, our names are Mr. And Mrs. Don Andrews. And yours are?"

"I'm Robert Green and this is my fiancée, Tammy Waring. We're getting married two weeks from tomorrow at that big church in Phoenix."

"C'mon in "they said as the gentleman unlocked and opened the door.

Tammy gasped in delight as she looked around the huge living room. 'This is so beautiful." She gasped.

Mrs. Andrews took over. "Come, let us show you the rest of the house. This is the master bedroom with it's own bath, the kitchen is next to it. It has a garbage disposal, a dishwasher, a refrigerator-freezer, lot's of cupboard space. Next to the kitchen is the other two bedrooms with a full bath between them. Naturally, it is all air-conditioned. There is a two-car garage with a laundry-room behind it. As you can see, we are both getting up in years and it was too much for us to handle anymore, so we had to buy a smaller home with less grounds"

"Oh, I just love it but I don't think we can afford it. What did you say you are asking for it?"

"We didn't say yet. But you look familiar. You said you are going to be married at the big church in Phoenix. Are you members there?"

"Yes, I guess you can call us that. Robert is the chairman .of the committee to build a ranch for street children. David Williams has donated land up by Lake Pleasant to build such a project."

"I thought I had seen you somewhere. We are members there also. I'm very interested in us becoming house parents, too."

"So, can we talk terms? Robert asked. Right now, we are in a state of transition. We both have jobs. Tammy has her own office at Motorola at a wonderful salary. I am employed by an automobile agency in Phoenix with a draw, etc. We expect to have a good income between us. The problem is we just don't have the cash at present.

"Don, may I take over for a few minutes. I feel like the Lord wants us to help these young people out. Tammy, I believe you can look forward to a long and happy relationship at Motorola. They're a good company to work for. Now what I want to suggest is that you let us carry the mortgage. That way you won't have to worry about how much down payment you have to make. Also, there won't be any high interest rates to contend with. Besides that you'd have to buy furniture and other items that we already have here. This furniture was too large to fit in our new home. I've had experience trying to sell used things and you can't begin to get back what it cost you. I propose that we include that in the purchase price gratis."

"You mean, you're *giving* it to us?"

"Yes."

Robert spoke: "So, if we accept your terms, what would the asking price be and how much a month would our payments be?"

"The first five years would be $1,000 a month. That would amount to sixty thousand dollars. The entire purchase price would be two hundred fifty thousand dollars. We could renegotiate at that time, if you wish. There would be no interest charged the first five years. Are you in agreement with all of this, Don?'

"Yes, you see, folks, she used to be a mortgage broker and she knows what she's talking about."

"Well, I've never been a mortgage broker or a banker but this sounds awfully good to me." Robert responded, "I say,' Yes', how about you, Tammy?"

"I am completely flabbergasted at the way God works

I say, yes, yes, yes!

"Okay. I have a contract here that we just have to fill in. How about us sitting down at the kitchen table and we'll finalize the deal right now. Can you come up with the first month's payment tonight?"

"I believe we can." Robert said. "You said, "one thousand dollars, right?"

"Yes, that will be fine. It's not necessary for us to have a first and last month's rent as this is a purchase rather than a rental."

"Who shall I make out the check to?"

"Make it out to Mrs. Mary Andrews."

"Thank you. Here you are."

"Now we'll fill out the rest of the agreement. The full purchase price including furniture is two hundred and fifty thousand dollars. Is that correct?"

"Yes it is." Robert confirmed.

"At the end of five years the balance will be one hundred ninety thousand dollars to be negotiated at that time. "

"Is that agreeable?"

"Yes, it is." Robert replied.

"Very well, If each of you will sign here and put today's date beside your name, I believe we have a contract."

She handed the papers over to Robert so that he and Tammy could sign."

Each of them signed their name and dated their signatures., then handed the papers back to Mary Andrews.

She separated them, keeping a copy for themselves and gave the other copy to Robert together with an envelope to place them in. He and Tammy rose Then Robert had another question. "It won't make any difference to the contract but I was wondering how much land there is. We never did discuss that."

"I'm sorry. I didn't even think of that phase of it. It is exactly one acre. You will, of course, get a survey of the property."

"Once again I'd like to say Thank You., Tammy declared. We never dreamed we'd find a house to rent, let alone one as gorgeous as this for such wonderful terms.

Thanks alone is hardly enough. We hope you will be present at our wedding. I also want you to meet my mother Martha Anderson who will be arriving on American airlines tomorrow. God bless you both!"

"I was just thinking, you should have a set of keys. Don, will you give her your keys to the house? We'll give you the other set when the deed is registered."

"Thank you. I'll want to bring my Mom over. She's going to love it."

"Will she be living with you?"

"No, she's having her furniture shipped out. We rented a house for her the other night. Her furniture will arrive Monday morning"

"We hope you'll come and visit us sometimes. We'd like to get to know you better."

"Great. We'd like that, too. We'll probably see you in church tomorrow morning.." Robert replied. We hate to go but we have so much to do and so little time to do it in. Saturday is our only time to do things together. But this time was worth it all! We do have to go now but we'll see you in church as the saying goes. God bless you both real good. Goodbye." He and Tammy walked out the door, got in the car. They couldn't wait till they got home to tell everybody the miracle God had just done for them. "It's past one o'clock. Do you want to stop and get some lunch somewhere?"

"I suppose we'd better. Howard and Ella have probably had lunch for themselves and the girls at least an hour ago"

"All right. There's a little sandwich shop around the corner. Let's stop there."

They pulled into a parking place and went in. How about a BLT? Howard asked.

"That sounds great! Maybe a glass of iced tea with it?"

"OK"

They really wanted to eat and get home. They were so anxious to tell everyone about their good fortune. As soon as their order came, Robert returned thanks, then each hurried to eat their sandwich. They took their tea along to drink in the car.

When they walked in the house, Howard and Ella began asking questions.

Robert said, Let's all sit down, where are the girls?

Call them, Ella. There's too much to tell to have to repeat it over and over again." Ella called them and they came bounding the stairs.

"Robert, you start."

"Well, God did a miracle for us today. We bought a house for $259,000 dollars. We paid a thousand dollars down and a thousand dollars a month for five years. That would amount to sixty thousand dollars. No interest, at the end of the five years, we can renegotiate if we desire. It's an acre of ground, beautifully landscaped, and a beautiful house with three bedrooms, and two baths. Somewhat like you have here except it's all on one floor. I'll let Tammy tell you the rest. "

"Well," said Tammy, there's this huge living room that is simply gorgeous, when you walk in the front door. Behind that, is the master bedroom and bath. Next to it is the kitchen; it has everything in it. Dishwasher, refrigerator-freezer, garbage disposal, the works. Next to the kitchen are two bedrooms with a bath between them. There is a large dining alcove at the back of the living room. A two-car garage with a laundry room behind it. Now, hold your breath!! The house is full of over-size furniture. Beautiful stuff. She said it was too large for their new house as it is a much smaller house. She threw all the furniture in. She said you couldn't get near what it was worth because it was considered used. They are financing the deal themselves so we don't have to qualify at a bank Her husband said she used to be a mortgage broker and knew what she was doing. Anyway, we signed the contract and have a copy of it. We'll get a deed to the property and a survey of the land. And I am overcome."

"When can we go see it? Tina asked

"Well, grandma will be here about 1:30. so we'll have to go and pick her up. I know she'll want to see it (we have a set of keys). So, we'll all go there together. Then we'll have to take her over to see her house. Her furniture should arrive sometime Monday morning She'll have to sleep with me Sunday night. I can't remember if I asked Bert Lansing to have the electricity turned on or not. Robert will help get her furniture in when it comes. He has her keys. Then we'll have to go somewhere and eat and I am pooped!"

"Wow! What a story! I told you, didn't I, Dorothy, that you couldn't out-give God! This is just one example."

CHAPTER FORTY-NINE

Following the Sunday Morning worship, they all went to the restaurant they had been going to for dinner, then went their way to the airport where they were to meet Tammy's mother. Her plane was delayed ten minutes so they all watched aircraft soaring and landing. Soon they heard the loud-speaker announcing her plane. They waited by the baggage pick-up. In a few minutes they saw her coming down the escalator. They ran down to meet her. Tammy hugged her and then turned to introduce her to the rest of the group. "Oh, Mom, I'm so glad you finally got here! We've only been here a couple of weeks but it seems like forever. Did you have anything to eat?"

"Yes, I picked up a couple of sandwiches and some cookies before I got on the plane. I ate them at noon and had a cup of coffee along with some potato chips that was furnished on the plane. I'll be just fine. There's one of my bags. " There's a larger one yet. There it is coming around."

Robert snatched them up and set them n front of her.

"Is that all? No, there's another large one that matches these. There it is now." Robert grabbed it as it came up. "Anything more?"

"No, that's all."

"Good! Howard will put them in the trunk of his car. Said Robert. He's pulling it up now. If the rest of you will wait out in front, I'll go get my car and pick the rest of you up. After Robert picked them up, Tammy turned to talk to her mother. "Mom, Robert is the one you talked to on the phone and he's going to be your new son-in-law."

"Hi, Mom," Robert said. "Glad to finally get to know you. No wonder you have such a beautiful daughter. You're a pretty good-looking woman yourself."

"Flattery will get you nowhere, young man but I must say, if I were a few years younger, I'd give her a run for her money."

"Huh, he replied, I can see now where she gets her teasing from. Ha! Ha! All kidding aside, we're glad you're finally here. After we drop your luggage off, we'll take you to see your new home. Hope you like it."

"I'm sure I will. How will we get in?"

"We have a set of keys the owner gave us."

"Trusting soul, isn't he? He wanted to know how old you are. I think he took a shine to Tammy and thought if you were anything like her, he might be interested."

"You didn't tell him, did you?

"Sure, why not?"

"Well, I never!"

"I think he was just a little bit older than you. So what?"

"Well, we'll just have to wait and see, won't we?"

"Yes, I guess so."

"Here's Howard's house. I'll take your luggage in and be right back."

Hopping back in the car, he said," New house, here we come." Cutting over a couple of streets to where her house was. "Here we are."

"Oh, how pretty!" she exclaimed, as she looked at the landscaping. "You say you have the keys? Let's go look inside."

They all piled out of their cars and followed Robert as he unlocked the door. Once inside there were exclamations of surprise. "Oh, it's lovely. I really like it and the rent is so reasonable, too. Let's look at the rest of the house. I feel like I could be really happy here and it's so close to Howard and Ella's place. I know I won't be lonely.

"No, you won't be lonely. Look down at the very end of this street. See that big house? That's where Robert and I will live." Tammy told her. "Shall we go down there and see that one, too?"

"Oh, goody," the girls cried. "I can't wait to see it."

They again piled into their cars and drove up in the driveway of Robert and Tammy's house. Robert went up and unlocked the door. Everyone stood in the doorway in shocked silence.

"Everything in here is yours? Tina asked in disbelief.

"Yep" Robert responded. "Everything!"

"The house, too, is yours?" asked Dorothy.

"And the land, a whole acre of it!"

"Wow! The Lord sure must love you a whole lot!"

"Yes, I think He does! Want to take a tour?"

"Lead the way," Howard and Ella responded.

Tammy took the lead. "You've seen the living room, notice the large dining alcove at the far end. As we go down this hall you'll see the master bedroom and bath. Next to it is the kitchen, which has a back door and the other two bedrooms with a bath between them and next to them is the door leading out to the two-car garage."

"Unbelievable!" Howard said.

"Yes, we could hardly believe it either. The payments are like rent, one thousand dollars a month for five years which would amount to sixty thousand dollars., all to be applied to the mortgage After that, we will negotiate the balance."

"What do you mean, renegotiate the balance?" asked Howard.

"Well, we might want to lower the monthly payments so we can invest in something else. I'm thinking especially of investing in the Children's ranch, which the church is intending to build. After all, it was our idea to start with and I think we should put our money where our mouth is, in a way of speaking."

"You know," her Mom replied. "I'm glad we didn't buy the other house. I might have different plans after we've been here a while."

"I have an idea what that might be but we'll wait a little while to see how everything works out. In the meantime you'll have a nice home to live in and close friends and family near you." Tammy said. "Now, if everyone is satisfied I'd like to go home, take a hot shower and go to bed. I am pooped."

"Aren't we going to have anything to eat?

"Oh, migosh!" cried Tammy. "I didn't realize we hadn't eaten yet. Would hamburgers be all right? There's a Burger King not very far from here."

"Anything will be OK with me, "Dorothy cried. I'm starved."
"You're always starved." Howard said with a grin.
"Then let's get rolling." Robert said. I'm a bit hungry myself."
They all piled into the cars and drove over to the Burger King. They decided to take everything home with them so they could eat in comfort. They were home to Howard's house in no time at all.

"You have a lovely house, too." Tammy's mom commented.

"Thank you." Ella said. Stay as long as you need to. We love having you. Tammy and Tina have been a joy to us."

"May I be excused now? I really want a hot shower and I do have to work tomorrow. Mom, Tina can show you where you'll sleep."

"You go right ahead. I'll be right behind you as soon as I finish this sandwich."

"OK Goodnight everybody." She said, tossing them a kiss.

"Just a minute." Robert cried. "Don't I get a kiss?

"You got one just like everyone else did

"Um-hmm. Then I'll take double next time."

"I'm too tired to argue." She walked around and kissed him."

"That's more like it! See you in the morning."

CHAPTER FIFTY

The next morning Robert was over to Howard's to pick Tammy's Mom up so he could take her over to her house as they had no idea when the moving van would be there. She needed time to decide where she wanted her furniture put. It would save a lot of time and moving things around if she could tell then where to put it. Ella had given her some rags to dust with. It was about ten o'clock when the moving van pulled up.

"Wow! That's pretty good timing." Robert said. He went out to see if he could help the movers. With Tammy's mom telling them where to put things, the rooms began to take shape nicely. "Gosh, it's beginning to look like home", she said. By noon, everything had been moved in and set in place.

"How about me taking you back to Howard and Ella's' for lunch? Do you want to come back here then or stay there for the rest of the day? I imagine you're pretty tired. I can bring you back here in the morning again and you can stay as long as you wish. I think on Tuesday night Tammy will want you to go shopping for your dresses. She still needs to get the flowergirl's dress, too. Two weeks from this Sunday will be the wedding and I think she needs to order flowers yet so you'll have plenty to help with. They're going to let us use the banquet room at the church for the reception. We think there'll be so many people who want to come that we're going to ask each one to bring a dish, salad or dessert. We'll have a sign-up-sheet for people to sign what they'll bring. Like that Idea?"

"Yes, that's a great idea. Who thought of that?"

Tammy and the Pharmacist

"Tammy. We knew we couldn't afford a big reception. This way anybody can come who wants to."

"I guess I will call it a day and go back over to Ella's when dinner was over I'd like to get a little bit more acquainted with her. They've sure been good to Tammy and Tina. I'm glad I'll be living close to them. By the way, will you be looking out for a good used car for me. Not too old but serviceable."

"I sure will. I've got to find one for Tammy, too. She's using Ella's car right now. But we can't afford to get one until pay-day as we used all our spare money to put the down payment on the house."

"Are you going to move in right away?"

"Oh, my, no! Not until I carry her over the threshold after the wedding. That's going to be our honeymoon right there! She won't have any vacation time for at least six months."

"Well, here we are at Ella's. I won't come in as I have some other things to do. I'll be over later this evening. Iris furnishes my meals. She'll begin to think I don't like her cooking so I'd better eat over there and come over later."

Tammy doesn't get home until five-thirty." Martha got out of the car and went in the house.

""Hi, I'm back. We have everything in place and dusted and ready to occupy. I will have to go grocery shopping and things like that. I asked Robert to look for a car for me. He says you will probably want to go shopping tomorrow night for our dresses and the flower girls. I think Tammy said something about forgetting to buy a veil. Did she say anything to you about it?"

"Yes, Tuesday night is the best night to shop. Every other night is filled up. Of course, now that they have the house, they won't need to go house-hunting anymore. It sure is a beautiful home."

"Yes, it is."

"Howard and the girls should be home soon for lunch. Are you hungry?

"I could eat my share, I think. They don't give you much to eat on a plane anymore. Can I help you with anything?"

"No, everything is ready. We're just waiting for them to get here. Oh, here they come now."

Tammy and the Pharmacist

"Hi, grandma," Tina cried. Boy, I'm glad you're here. Are we gonna sleep in your new house tonight?"

"No. I need to get some groceries and cleaning supplies first, and I didn't get the dishes or linens unpacked yet. I'll do that tomorrow. Robert will take me over there in the morning. You know, Ella, maybe I could take a sandwich along and a bottle of iced tea. Then Robert won't need to pick me up until supper time."

"Would you like to go grocery shopping this evening, then? I can use the car tonight because Tammy doesn't have anyplace special to go tonight. She can stay home and rest."

"Yes, that would be wonderful."

"OK that's what we'll do then,

As soon as they finished dinner, Martha and Ella left the kitchen for Howard and the girls to clean up. Ella took her to a big Wal-Mart Superstore. They were through shopping by 9 o'clock and went to Martha's house to put them away. Ella put the frozen stuff in the freezer and loaded the other perishables in the refrigerator. Martha put the canned goods in the cupboard. Soon everything was put away and she locked the door and they headed for Ella's house.

If you don't mind, I think I'll take a shower and go to bed." Martha said.

"You go right ahead. I think I will, too. See you in the morning."

The next morning, Robert picked Martha up right after breakfast and took her over to her house. Now that she had food in the house and ice in the refrigerator, she could fix lunch for herself. She put sheets on the beds and towels in the bathroom and the house began to look lived in. Then she heard a knock at the door and saw a man standing there "Hello, she said, "May I help you?"

"I'm Burt Lancaster, the owner of this house. I take it you're the one who is renting it?"

"Yes, I'm Martha Andrews\\ That was my daughter you talked to. Won't you come in?" she said holding the screen door open.

"You've really got settled quick, haven't you?"

"Yes, my daughter's young man helped me a lot. They're getting married a week from Sunday at that big church in Phoenix. Maybe you'd like to go. They're having a big reception right after the wedding in the recreation center. All you have to do is bring something for the dinner, like a bag of potato chips or a jar of pickles. That way, everybody who wants to can come. Isn't that a good idea?"

"Sure is! Do you have a way to get there?'

"Not yet. My daughter's fiancé is looking for one for me. He's a car salesman. We've just been so busy we haven't had time to look for one yet."

"May I offer you a lift? I just live on the street behind you. I can do your yard work for you, too."

"That's wonderful. And thank you for your offer to take me to the church. Can you take me this Sunday, too?

Howard has his family to take and that would be a help to them, too."

"I sure could. I've been thinking I ought to go to church but I didn't know anybody there."

"Well, this is a good time to start. Thank you for offering. What about your wife? Will she go too?"

"Oh, my wife died a little over five years ago. I've been living alone ever since."

"Oh, I'm sorry to hear that, although I lost my husband about that time, too. You know, I almost forgot. I owe you some money, too. Five hundred dollars, isn't it?"

"Yes, but I didn't come over for that. We can wait awhile if you need it."

"No, I have the money from the sale of my house

It's no hardship and I thank you for waiting. "Here you are," as she handed him the check.

"Anything you need just call me. Here's my card with my phone number on it."

"I don't have a phone number yet but I'll give it to you when I get one."

"Would you like me to call the phone company for you? I have your name on your check and I know this address like the back of my hand"

"Why, yes, that would be wonderful. I surely do appreciate it."

"O.K. then, I'll be on my way."

"Thank you again. You're welcome anytime."

By the time he left, it was noon so she decided to sit down and have a sandwich and a glass of iced tea. Then watched her favorite Christian program on TV. Knowing they would be going on a shopping trip after dinner, she decided to lie down and take a nap. She had been napping for about an hour when she heard the phone ring. Going out to the living room to pick it up, she heard a man say, "Mrs. Andrews?

"Yes, it is'

"This is the telephone company, I understand you want your phone connected."

"That's right".

"You live at 1761 Murphy St. in Glendale? "

"That's right".

"Well, as of right now, you are connected. Your phone number is .399-1761.

"Do you have that?"

"Yes, I do. Thank you very much.

"WOW Will I have a lot to tell Ella when I get back there. I had her phone number but I can't remember what I did with it. Guess I'll have to look it up in the phone book."

Robert came to pick her up a little before five.

"Boy, have I ever had a day" she said.

"Oh? What happened"

"The nicest man came to see if I needed anything. Said he would mow or weed or anything else I needed. I learned he was a widower and that he used to live here. I paid him the rest of the security deposit and he called the phone company and had my phone hooked up for me."

"Well, wasn't that nice of him."

"Not only that but he's going to take me to church Sunday and go to the wedding, too."

"Hmm you sure make hay while the sun shines, don't you?"

"I really didn't try to get information out of him. When he offered to pick me up for church, I naturally asked him if his wife was going, too, he said she'd been dead for over five years. And then I told him about the wedding and he said he'd like to go. I think he's been awfully lonely."

"Well I can see that won't be a problem for you. I think Tammy is a chip off the old block."

"Why whatever do you mean?' she said with a grin.

"You know very well what I mean. I think I'll have to tell Tammy to keep an eye on you."

"Don't you dare!"

"Well, I guess you'll be busy tonight getting your wedding finery. Ella has to get hers, too. See you later. Bye"

Martha ran in the house to see if Ella had been able to reach the parents of the little girl the pastor had recommended for the flower girl.

" Hi! Glad you're home. I got in touch with the mother of the little girl who's to be flower girl. She is going to meet us at the bridal shop so we can get those things done first. I think Tammy will want to get white satin shoes, and her veil there, too. Where do you usually get your good dresses?"

"In New York we usually went to Macy's or J. L. Hudson, but I don't know about the stores here. Is there a J. C. Penny here?" I like their dresses, especially the petites. I'm so short."

'So, how did your day go?"

"Oh, OK. I hear a 'but' coming. What happened?"

"Well, this man came over and I learned he was the owner of my house so I wrote him out a check for the balance we owed. Then I told him about Robert and Tammy's wedding and that he could go if he wanted to, all he needed to do was bring a bag of potato chips or a large jar of pickles. So he's coming this Sunday, too, and wants to pick me up. He also called the phone company and they installed my phone. How's that?"

"I knew it! I just knew it. Ask Tammy if I didn't say I thought he was interested in you! Here she comes now."

"What are you two gossiping about now?"

"Your mother's got her a boy friend, that's what!"

"Mom, what is she talking about."

"I'll tell you on the way. We have too much to do right now.'

When they reached the Bridal Shop, they found Mrs. Lawson and Cindy waiting for them.

Tammy and the Pharmacist

"Good evening, Mrs. Lawson and Cindy, too. Shall we go inside?"

Inside they spoke to the lady who was to wait on them.

Cindy is to become the flower girl in my wedding. We have our dresses in lay-a-way and will take them home with us tonight. We'd like to have them brought out so we can find a matching dress for Cindy.

"What is your name, please?

Tammy Waring."

Just a moment, please."

Your salesgirl isn't in. I'll bring some small dresses in.

I believe the junior bridesmaids are lilac and pink. I'll see what I can find to coordinate with them. Do you object to a print?"

"Please bring several out and we'll choose from them".

"Yes, ma'am."

"Soon she came back with several small dresses. There was one that was lilac print on a pink background. Let her try that one on," Tammy asked.

It fit her beautifully, "We'll take it, Tammy said. "Now, do you have white satin slippers? I'd like to see something in an 8 medium. Also, I forgot the buy a veil. Do you have anything styled like a picture hat?

"Let's see, white satin slippers and a veil. I'll be right back."

"Here we are. Let's try these on. She took Tammy's other shoes off and slipped the white ones on.

Tammy stood up to see how they felt. They were just right. Now, the hat. She stepped over in front of the mirror and adjusted it on her head. "It fits just right! Let's try the veil down. Oh, I do like that. Do you have children's shoes here."

"Sorry. No"

"That's OK. We can get those just about anywhere. Will you please wrap these together with the others we have in lay- away and let us know the balance due."

"Mom," Tammy said in an aside. Can you let me have a thousand?"

Martha replied. "Of course. I should have given it to you before we came."

The clerk came in with the package. Let's see. The total comes to $1,497.50 including tax. You paid $500down.

"That leaves a balance of Nine hundred ninety-seven dollars and fifty cents."

"Here you are. She handed her the check. She turned to Mrs. Lawson.,"Can you get her the black patent leather shoes? "You can take her dress," she said, as she handed her the package."

We have more shopping to do tonight."

"Yes, of course."

"We'll take our leave then and see you in church Sunday (or Thursday) before the rehearsal on Saturday."

"Well, where shall we shop for your Mother of the Bride and Mother of the Groom dresses?"

"How about J. C. Penney? Or Beall's?"

"Let's try J. C. Penney first, OK?" Martha suggested.

They jumped out of the car, locked the door and hurried inside. "Do either of you know your sizes? Petite or regular? Petites are in one location and misses in another," said Tammy.

"I wear a petite size 8," Martha said.

"I also wear a petite in an 8 or 10."

"Fine. Tammy said. These are petites right over here".

"Oh, look at this one. It will go beautifully with Lilac."

"Let's see, the Matron of Honor is wearing lilac, she's blonde so the Mother of the Bride should wear pink, I think.

"How about trying some on to see how they look?" If you don't find what you want here, we can try Dillard's or Beall's.

"I don't really see any here that I like. Let's try Dillard's. It's right next door.

"Okay. Let's go!"

"They walked right in to the ladies department and found petites. Let's look for sizes as well as color. OK"

"Here are quite a number of eights. I like something sleeveless. What do you think, Martha?"

"I'm trying to visualize "

"Well, try some on. They usually look different when you have then on. How about this one?" She'd picked out a pink sheer with lace that draped across the bosom." Martha went into a dressing room to try it on."

When she came out to show it to them she got a few wolf-whistles from bystanders. That did it! She decided on that one. Then Ella picked one out from the rack in lilac and went in to try it on. When she came out there were more wolf whistles. Laughing, they decided that the woods were full of whistlers but just ignored them. Now their shopping was done except for shoes. They went over to look at them but found them too extreme, so they went back to J. C. Penney's and looked there. They had a nice assortment, so they finally found a pair for each of them. They were ready to come home. When they came in the door Howard and Robert wanted a peek, but Tammy said, "nothing doing." Anyway, I'm too pooped to pop and I'm going to bed."

Howard looked abused but Tammy was adamant. "This makes an awfully long day for me and I just have to get to bed."

Robert looked abused, too, but no one paid him any attention. It wouldn't be long and he'd be getting all the attention he wanted.

"I guess that's about everything. We just have to do the flowers now. And plan what we'll take to the reception. Having it at the church sure takes a lot of work off us. Thank the Lord."

CHAPTER FIFTY-ONE

THE WEDDING

The church was beautifully decorated with red roses tied with a big white satin bow attached to each pew for about five rows back. A beautiful arch graced the pulpit area where the bride and groom would stand.

Pastor 'Bob" Harrington, Robert Green and Howard Peters came out of the small room which adjoined the sanctuary and advanced to the Center aisle, as the organist began to play the Wedding March from Lohengrin They watched as the flower girl began to toss rose petals from her basket, followed by the two Junior bridesmaids. Then the Maid of Honor began to make her trek to the altar, her bouquet of yellow roses contrasted beautifully with her lilac dress. When she had taken her place beside the others, Robert stepped forward and began to sing.:

"Because you come to me with naught save love
And hold my hand and lift mine eyes above,
A wider world of hope and joy I see
Because you come to me."

Then Tammy responded:

Because you speak to me in accents sweet,
I find the roses waking round my feet
And I am led through tears and joy to thee
Because you speak to me.

They then sing together:

Because God made thee mine,
I'll cherish thee through light and darkness
Through all time to be.
And pray His love may make our love divine
Because God made thee mine!"

Pastor: "Who giveth this woman in marriage?"

Martha stood to her feet: "I, her mother, do."

Pastor: "Will you, Robert and Tammy take each others hands and repeat after me. I, Robert do promise to love and cherish you until the Lord calls me home. Robert repeated after him.

Tammy, repeat after me. I do promise to love and cherish you until the Lord calls me home. Which Tammy repeated after him, May we have the rings, please? Howard handed him the rings. Robert repeat after me With this ring I, thee, wed. Robert repeated after him and slipped her ring on her finger. Tammy repeat after me, With this ring I thee wed. Tammy repeated his words and then slipped his ring on his finger.

Pastor: Under the laws of this land which I am required to uphold, I now pronounce you man and wife. You may kiss the bride. (Robert didn't have to be told twice! Folding his arms around her he kissed her long and hard.) I present to you, Mr. And Mrs. Robert Green. The organist pealed out the recessional as they proceeded down the aisle followed by their attendants to form a receiving line at the end of the aisle.

Those who were taking charge of the dinner in the banquet hall slipped out of their places and hurried to their posts. Several hundred people had responded to the invitation to participate in it and the tables were heaped bountifully. The photographers were busily taking pictures of the wedding party.

As they folded up their equipment, Robert and Tammy went down the stairs to join the friends who had stayed for the reception. After a decent interval, they stole away to their new home where Robert gathered his bride in his arms and carried her over the threshold.

Meanwhile, Tina was a little disturbed at her sudden change in status. Tammy had tried to make her understand that it was only temporary for that week. Of course, Dorothy was happy to have her pal a little bit longer since she would begin to live in the new house with Robert and Tammy after their brief honeymoon period. And it was brief! On Thursday evening they all met again at the church for the committees to begin to function .Since Robert was the head chairman, he wanted to get all the committees in full swing, especially the ones who were to approach businesses and wholesalers in the area to see how many items they would donate to the project.

To see what and how all this will be accomplished we invite you to follow building the ranch, in the sequel which follows this one, THE HACIENDA OF HAPPINESS AND HOPE a chronicle of hope and despair as they endeavor to find the means to build their dream for the boys and girls without homes. Not only does it get done but Sarah finds her way out there, too. Look for it soon.! You won't want to miss it!

Printed in the United States
103958LV00004B/443/A